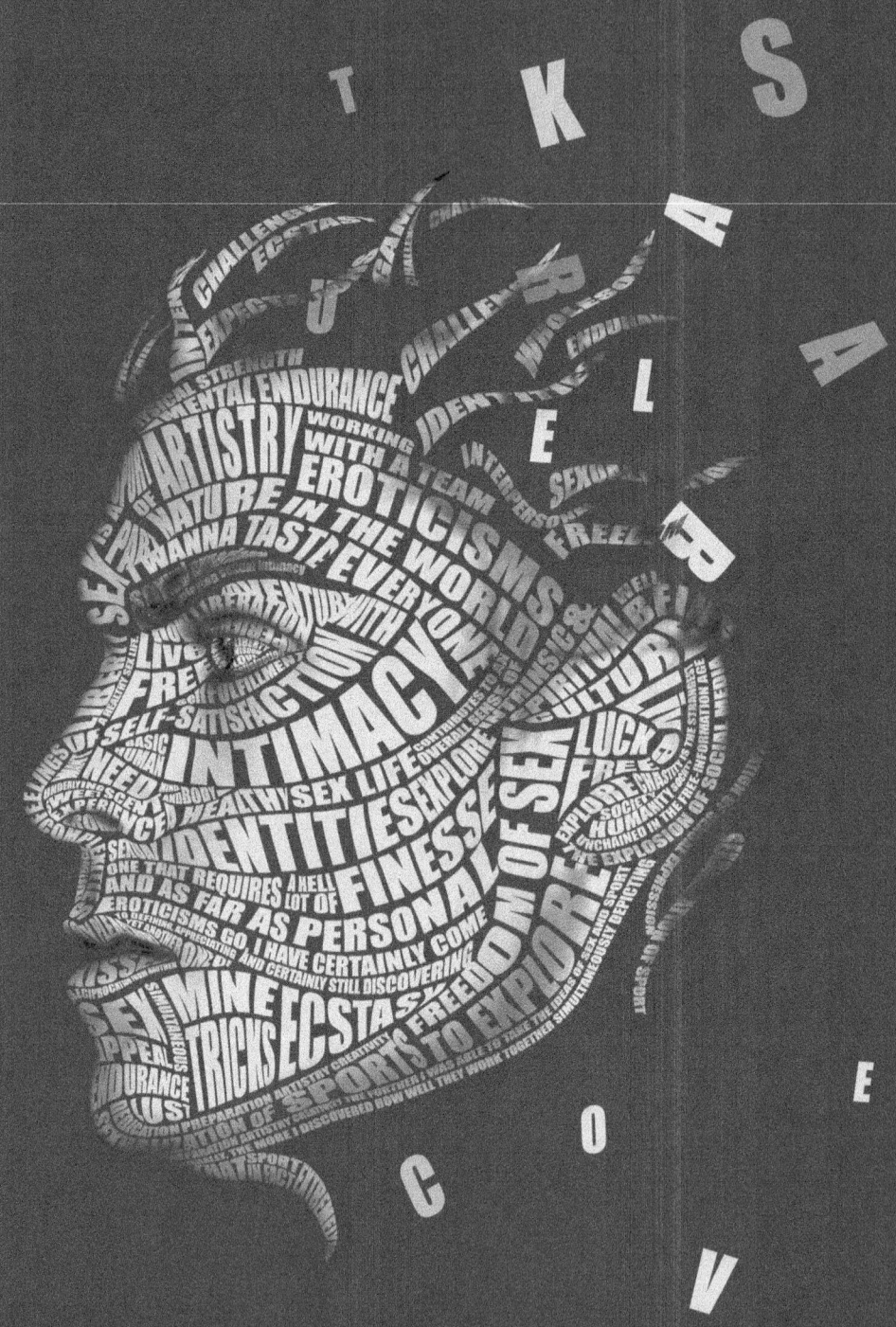

Sex, like life is a journey of self discovery - Kaleb Cove

SEX. It's a painstakingly simple yet indefatigable three letter word, but as a society we are confronted with it daily. Everyone does it, yet somehow no one wants to talk about it. It's high time that for humanity's sake, we face up to our sexual identity and grow a pair. For any true progress in gender tolerance and sexual acceptance, we must first understand enough about ourselves, in order to even attempt to understand the hearts and minds of others.

I'm inspired by the unwillingness to conform to the belief that sexuality in the modern age is true to human nature, when history is literally painted rich with demonstrations of the true sexual potential represented by societies past. Sexuality is the one thing that makes all of us alike and I'm driven by the potential to draw attention to the importance of our sexuality and contribute to the shifting global paradigm of sexual awareness and acceptance.

Sex is an individual journey and what Im trying to achieve with the Kaleb Sutra is to give you a glimpse into some of mine. On the off chance that you may learn something from it, I hope that you may in the least draw on some of my experiences and have some fun along the way.

If the average male does in fact think about sex once every seven seconds, surely we could speak about it once in a while.

"I think it's funny that we were freer about our sexuality in the 4th Century BC. It's a little bit disconcerting"
– Angelina Jolie

When I was fifteen, I knew everything about sex.

At eighteen, I thought I knew it all.

And in my twenties, I've realized I have so much more to learn.

Pisces natare oportet

STARTING POSITIONS

By Kaleb Cove

DEDICATION

As I'm about to enter into my tenth season of broken ribs, and nearing the end of the first season with a new teammate, the starting of these positions would not have kicked off without the post game evenings in front of a palm-shaped horizon, overlooking the world.

From Kythira to la Punta del Este (& apparently Sydney), we both know that some of the best games are played whilst travelling. How good.

To take it all back to the beginning, GMS, you gave me "the" waterbed and an open book, and for that reason I'm (finally) finishing writing my first one. *non sum oblitus.*

Fr. M. M, for teaching me that in order to find myself, I must undertsand that it is all how it was meant to be. *fac recte et nil time.*

To the M games played and the next M, take your positions.

PPPBG. PitchyP Et. S.

TABLE OF CONTENTS

THE KICK OFF

"Our organic drives and urges are never separable from
the search for meaning and the question for communion."
– James B. Nelson

I ndeed, every sexual experience is a journey, and every sexual fantasy
tells a story. This first installment of the Kaleb Sutra touches on
an exploration of my sexual identity, and this collection of short
stories illustrates some of the dynamics that develop during the
path of exploring sexual intimacy.

My journey of self-discovery, as I have learned over my relatively
few years of sexual activity, promotes a level of personal freedom,
which is built on—and has resulted, again, in—feelings of deep self-
fulfillment and liberation. Our sexual identity is often obscured;
without question, unhealthy to both mind and body. Our sexuality
is a deep-seated basic need of human function and in essence is a big
part of who we are. It affects our underlying self-satisfaction with
life, as well as the subsequent associated, extrinsic perceptions.
These complexities—at large and in the specific minutiae, ultimately
define the physical relationships we develop and maintain with
others. I'm not the first to say this:

"I need more sex, OK? Before I die I wanna taste everyone
in the world." – Angelina Jolie

"Sex is a part of nature. I go along with nature."
– Marilyn Monroe

A healthy sex life contributes to an overall sense of intrinsic
and spiritual well-being. Put simply, it makes us feel good about
ourselves. It motivates us to take pride and care in personal health
and appearance, if for no other reason than to appeal to new sexual
partners and keep the "spark" alive with current ones.

But just as important as the instinct of connecting sexually with our sexual partners is this:

> "One half of the world cannot understand the pleasures
> of the other." – Jane Austen

And absolutely this:

> "The greatest pleasure in life is doing what people say you
> cannot do." – Walter Bagehot

So true. And in the spirit of that achievement, I have set out to do some of the things that others only ever imagine, so I can share them with you. In the end there exists above all a relevant, almost desperate need to be desired. Establishing and maintaining a personal status-quo of positive self worth runs deepest to this underlying need. This is the font, the source, the drive. As long as, that is, reciprocation from another continues the positive cycle, thereby bringing the whole paradigm around full circle, and highlighting the importance of maintaining a healthy sex life.

> "There may be some things better than sex, and there may
> be some things worse. But there's nothing exactly like it."
> – W.C. Fields

History is literally painted rich with cross-cultural, cross-racial, cross-generational, cross-gender, "cross-any taboo" sexual paradigms. The exploits of the Romans perhaps depict most generously the concept of the movement of sexual libertarianism. (The Greeks in their Golden Age were excellent models, as well.)

> "I think it's funny that we were freer about our sexuality in
> the 4th Century BC. It's a little bit disconcerting"
> – Angelina Jolie

Long story short: Freedom of sexual expression has for the bulk of human history been the widely and socially accepted norm. So answer me this simple question, when did it all go wrong?

Consider this at your leisure, however. The Moral of this collection of short stories is the importance (better, the freedom) of taking a look at the current shifts in social trends towards sex itself, moving in fact backwards! Indeed, back toward those core values established by the Greeks and Romans. After Rome, the Dark Ages. Then the Renaissance, the Reformation, Pietism, American Protestantism, the sexual revolution; pigeonhole history as you will. In recent years, each subsequent generation has represented a greater and greater willingness to increase the presence and freedom of sex in daily life. Mainstream media, the pervasiveness of the internet, the explosion of social media and networking; now it is such that you're able to—at will—find exactly what you are looking for, however "wholesome" to some, however "perverse" to others. Humanity at large, unchained in the free-Information Age, is becoming more open and willing (if nothing else, less hindered) to explore their sexuality, giving us more freedom to explore and develop our individual sexual identities.

"Of all the sexual aberrations, chastity is the strangest."
– Jacques Thibault

We each have our personal eroticisms, and the freedom to explore and develop these is key to self-gratification. I certainly have plenty, and this little collection of mine has drawn me into a new exploration of sexual expression; specifically, here, the concurrency of the themes of sex and sport. Sport combines elements of physical strength with mental endurance. At its best at levels of the highest artistry. (Much like the best sex, wouldn't you agree?) It forces us into situations that involve working as a team, as well as successfully playing against an opponent and sometimes a skilled combination of both. In a lot of ways this reflects the basic virtues and interpersonal challenges underlying and underpinning sex. It's an experience filled with intensity and passion, combined with expectations, intensely personal and sensitively interpersonal. Therefore driven by individual need and desire while at the same time requiring individual humility and recognition for the mutual experience. Underlying it all, one always must avail themselves of somewhat predefined rules and processes and incorporate them (in the ideal) into a "journey" of both the self and other.

"Sex is emotion in motion" – Mae West

Sport icons have been highly sexualized, even so much as revered as 'gods' in their own professional glory. From the Ancient Romans, to modern sports stars like David Beckham, these 'gods of sport' are put on a pedestal and observed for their sex appeal, in collaboration with their sporting prowess, drawing these two themes even closer together.

A closer look at the sexualization of sports has inspired me to take this a little further and render a personal interpretation of the two, thus creating this first installment of the Kaleb Sutra. I would strongly argue that sex is in fact a sport and one that requires a hell of a lot of finesse, precision, dedication, endurance, preparation, artistry, creativity, freedom, teamwork… and so much more. The further I was able to take the ideas of sex and sport literally, the more I discovered how well they work together, simultaneously depicting that sport is in fact extremely sexy, and as far as personal eroticisms go, I have certainly come very close to defining, appreciating and certainly still discovering yet another one of mine. All that's left is for it to be put in print.

"Friends, you are lucky you can talk about what you did
as lovers; the tricks, laughter, the words, the ecstasy."
– from the Vidya (c. 700-1050)

CHAPTER 1

BASEBALL

You looked hot enough to make any guy want to do really naughty things to you, the way you ran around the field in that particularly tight-fitting uniform. You must have worn that same uniform for a number of years because you seem to have grown into it, and now as a tall, athletic, and muscular nineteen-year-old you fill it perfectly in all the right places. Your pants sit tight, especially around the top of your thighs, barely able to conceal the massive package your cup is forced to hide. Every time I start staring at your perfectly formed ass, your perky cheeks so small and tight, I find myself falling straight back into that same fantasy I always have about wanting you to catch every last drop of what I'm pitching.

I get you alone in the locker room. Watching you strip out of your gear makes me want to get naked with you. I watch you lean up against one of the lockers butt naked, your long, athletic legs and semi-excited cock inviting me over. I waste no time slamming you up against the locker and pressing my body into yours. Skin on skin, I slide my hand between your toned thighs while running my tongue around your stiff left nipple, gently nibbling it, to your delight. Your thick teenage meat hardens in the palm of my hand like a baseball bat and fills both my hands quickly. I start circling your swelling knob with the tips of my fingers, as it fast covers my hands with your sticky teenage juice

DOUBLE PLAY

My hands find their way in between your legs and I'm irresistibly drawn to what I discover there. Almost by themselves, my fingers gently slide into the smooth, slightly moist hole they encounter, and you start to breathe heavily as I work my way deeper inside you, my hard pole impatiently poking into your stomach. You lick your lips seductively, inviting me to put it somewhere else. I throw you onto the ground and mount you backwards so that your moistening hole is staring me in the face. At the same time I feel my throbbing inches slide straight to the back of your throat and you obediently swallow me whole, unable to breathe. My mouth is wrapped around your hole, my tongue piercing your puckered rim as my hands force your cheeks apart, preparing them for what's about to come next.

Both playmates cop a mouthful = mutual satisfaction!

Difficulty: medium

HIGH AND TIGHT

aggressively tear my swollen knob from the back of your throat and tell you to get up and lie on your side on the bench in front of me. Still on my knees, I grab your feet and shoulders, and without warning, press my spit-covered cock against your spread cheeks, slowly sliding inside you watching your jaw clench as you feel me penetrate you, inch by inch. I pull our bodies tightly together and forcefully thrust myself in and out of you, feeling your smooth, athletic body pleasure me eagerly.

Unique sideways insertion + penetration
can provide intense stimulation
Penetration: deep
Difficulty: medium

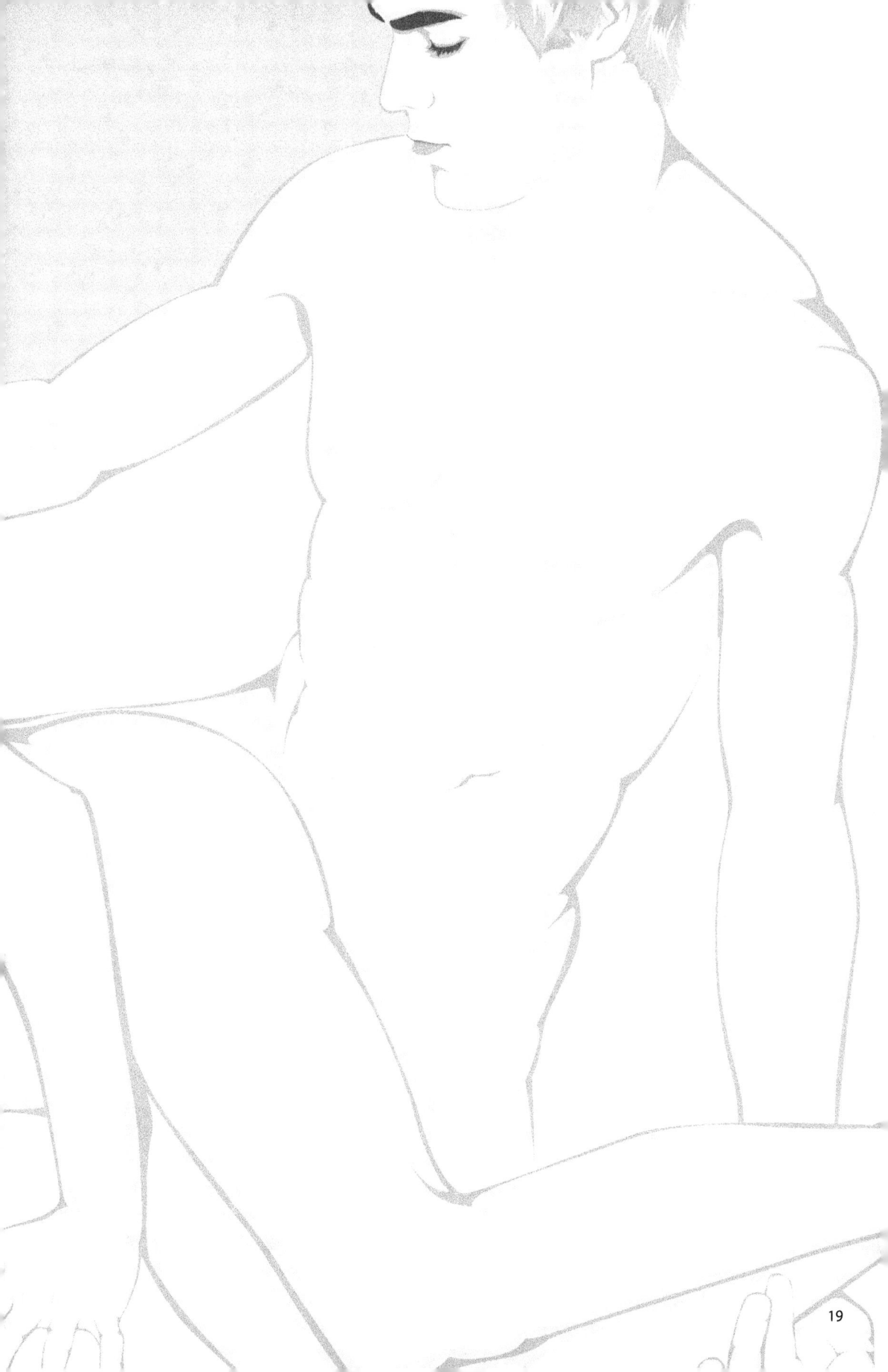

PITCHER S MOUND

t gets even hotter when you climb on top. I sit up on the bench after pulling out of you and guide you down on top of me. You tease me with your legs spread just wide enough for me to see my cock and your tight ass glistening between them. I wrap my hand around your throbbing cock and stroke it while my other hand fingers you. You slide around my pulsing pole, teasing my knob with your sticky hole. You let it slide into you just far enough for it to throb even harder with anticipation. I can feel my teasing head excite you until you cant take the suspense anymore and let it slide inside you, groaning as my massive cock impales you to the core. You grab my hair and start to ride me, so deep I can feel you stretch wider and wider apart with each thrust. It's time to flip you around, so I can sit back and enjoy the view.

Role reversal -
Bottom is on top +
in control

Penetration: deep
Difficulty: medium

SCORING POSITION

Standing in front of me, you spread your tight cheeks apart and force me to admire how well I'm using your hole. Impressed with how good your ass looks after my eight-plus inches have been inside you, I grab those cheeks and pull you back down on top of me. From here I can watch you gliding up and down on my full length. Each time you manage to pull my cock right to the edge of your hole, and I watch you slide all the way back down it again. I'm rock hard and cock-deep inside you and you're almost frantic with lust as my knob suddenly swells and starts to gush in torrents, filling you completely. You jam down on top of me even harder, until my load starts dripping out of you and running back down my hard pole, sticky and reeking of your teenage scent.

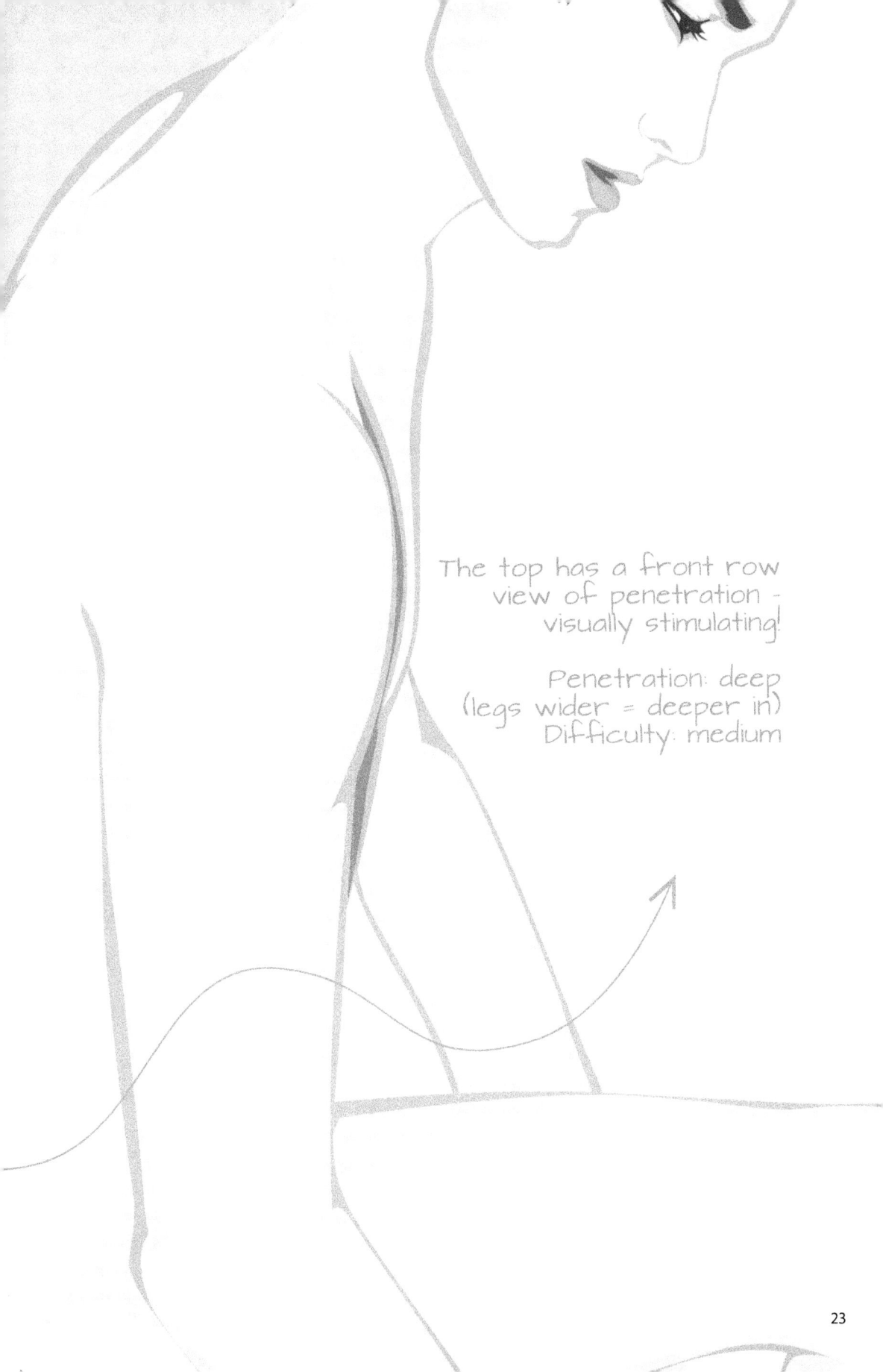

The top has a front row
view of penetration -
visually stimulating!

Penetration: deep
(legs wider = deeper in)
Difficulty: medium

GRAND SLAM

lift you off my tingling cock only to hear you beg me to thrust back inside you. You want more? I'm still throbbing hard and aching to go again. I push you face down on the ground and enter you from behind, instantly sinking my thick cock fully into you. Squatting down, I force-fuck you with hard, full-body thrusts from my waist. Each time I slam into you, your breath gets caught in your throat as if you've just been hit by a fastball. I'm pumping you so hard now that you barely manage to beg me to give you something else stuck down the back of your throat. I grab your shoulders and push into you one last time, as I feel my balls tense up, ready to blow again.

Powerful thrust from the waist means greater intensity

Penetration: deep
Difficulty: easy

DOUBLE HEADER

You beg me to let you taste me, and just as I feel my knob starting to drip, I pull your lips apart with two fingers and jam my bursting head into your mouth, barely in time for you to feel me spill my second hot load. I feel you licking my tingling foreskin, sucking up every last drop. Seconds later, I have your throbbing cock in my mouth. I choke on your thick knob as you plunge deep into me, copiously dripping down the back of my throat, generously repaying the favour.

intense finishing position &
total mutual satisfaction!

Difficulty: easy

CHAPTER 2

BASKETBALL

Probably my favorite teenage fantasy had a lot to do with a certain Joel, the jock Captain of my highschool basketball team. He would yell at me to keep my head down, and, "Pound that ball harder down the court!" I would do exactly as he ordered, occasionally double dribbling on purpose, just to have him run over and throw himself up against me in his sweat-covered singlet, breathing heavily in my face, barking at me to lift my game.

Every one of those vivid sexual fantasies from the high school basketball team hit me at once when you put me flat on my ass on the basketball court behind my place one Saturday afternoon. You had so swiftly managed to steal the ball from me, that as I looked up at you I instantly saw Joel standing over me, high-top basketball sneaker pinning my chest and grinning down at me, taunting me to finally make a move. I could smell the scent of teenage sweat, from your sneaker all the way up your loose shorts, which were already sporting a semi-flaccid slab of teenage enthusiasm.

I didn't waste a second, and reached up and pulled your shorts down to your ankles, hardening you to a complete stiff as I wrapped my hand around it and began to jerk you off. It wasn't long till my hand was as sticky as your knob, and your hand slid over and furiously started playing with mine. I was on the ball with your keen sense of adventure, as you grabbed onto my hand and pushed it down between your legs, insisting that I finger you. Without a second thought I obliged, your tight ass dripping with sweat and waiting for me to slide inside. Forcefully, two fingers turned to three, and once I'd broken in your keen little ass, my cock began to drip with its own sticky mess, impatiently anticipating the slam dunk that was finally about to take place.

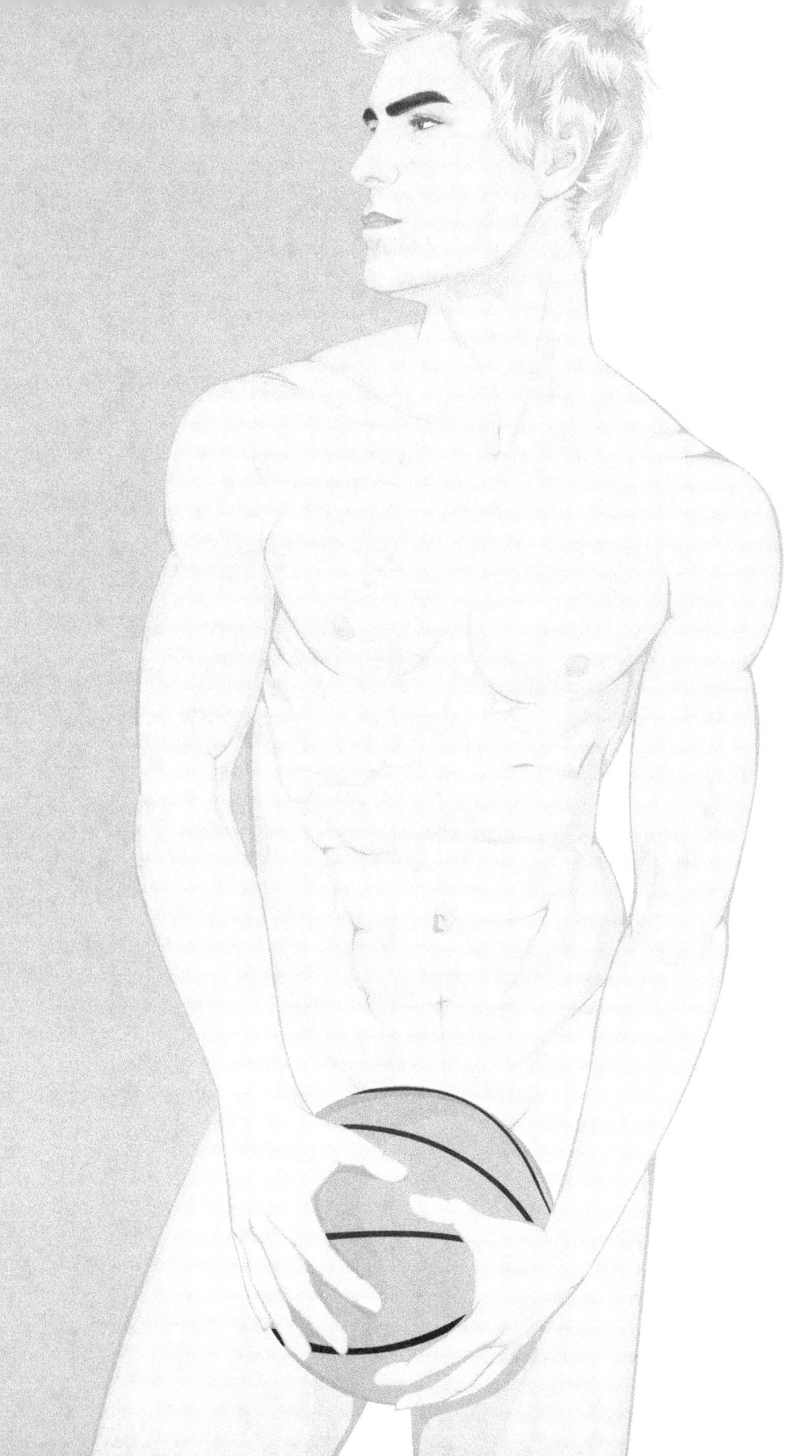

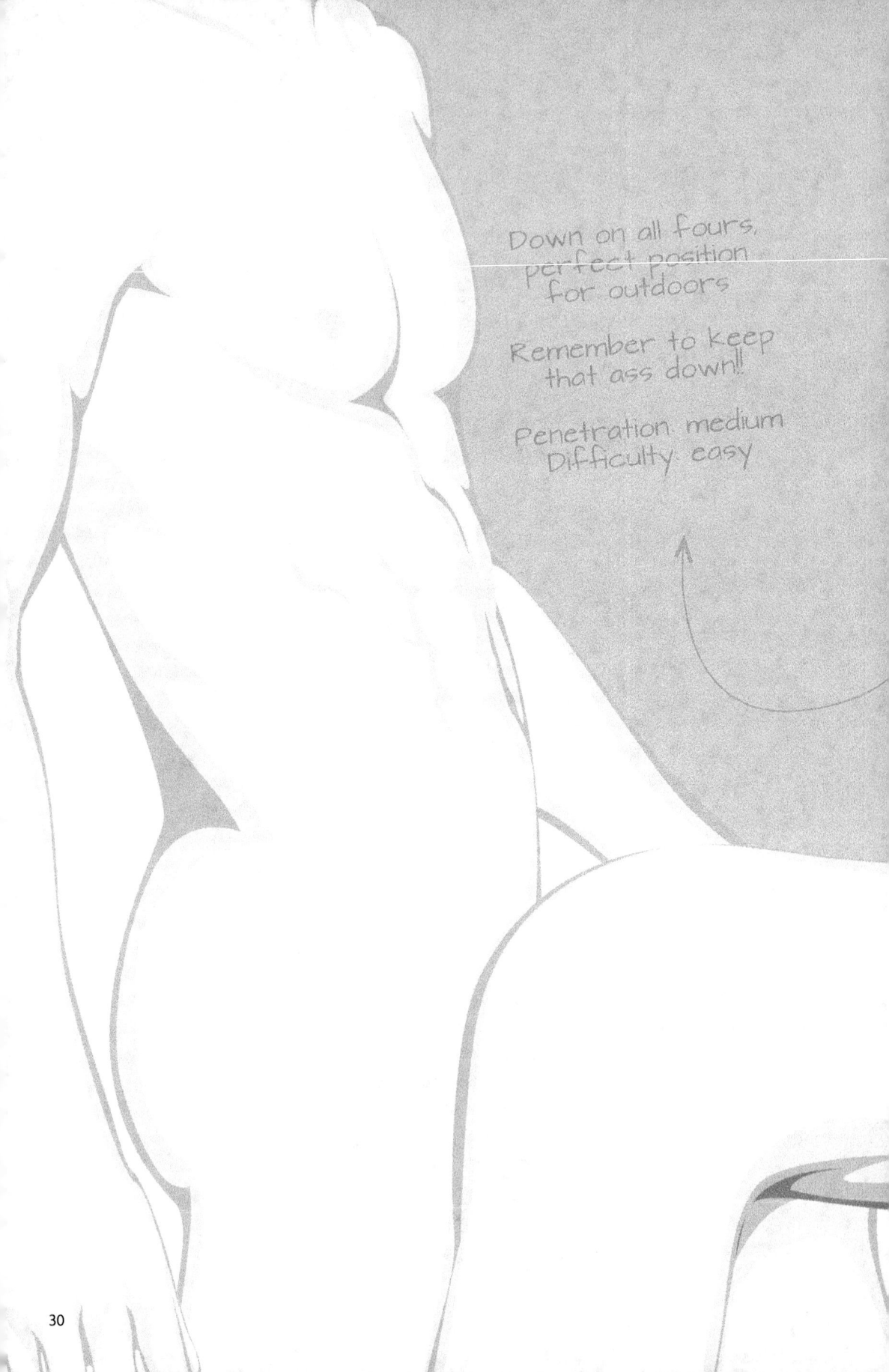

Down on all fours,
perfect position
for outdoors

Remember to keep
that ass down!!

Penetration: medium
Difficulty: easy

POWER FORWARD

You more than hinted that you were ripe and ready for my three fingers to be replaced with something a lot bigger, flipping over and rising on all fours in front of me. I was horny as hell and more than willing to oblige. I dropped to my knees behind you, eager to satisfy your teenage cravings. I slapped you around a couple of times with my big cock and watched your puckered lips tighten in front of me in anticipation. As I began to push myself into you, I realized it was going to be a tight squeeze. This was definitely your first in a while, and it was going to be like breaking you in all over again. Despite the conflicted look of both anticipation and hesitation on your face, you pouted your smooth ass out toward me, telling me that, yes, you wanted it bad.

FULL COURT PRESS

My appetite was growing rapidly, and I didn't hesitate dropping you onto your stomach, aggressively pressing you onto the surface of the basketball court I was about to destroy your ass on. As you flattened under me and spread your legs apart, I planked myself on top of you, pinning you down, and slowly eased into you from behind. I felt your sweat covered butt relax just enough to let me to push further inside. You opened your legs wider and invited me in further, as you started to enjoy the stretching from my thick, throbbing cock, inching deeper inside. I gladly obliged, feeding you my smooth knob, nearly half way in now. I feel you run one of your hands up my thigh and watch closely as you grab your left cheek, eagerly ripping it aside, desperate to feel my last few inches fill you.

Put some clothes/towel on a rough surface first! Spreading cheeks = deeper penetration

Penetration: medium
Difficulty: easy

Rough riding
(role reversal)

Penetration: deep
Difficulty: easy

GIVE AND GO

I lie back and let you satisfy your craving, as you take control over my rock hard pole, standing at full mast, so ready for you to inch the rest of your way down it. As your legs nervously shake, in a single movement you force your little ass as far down as you can go, and take me all the way in. Your breathing intensifies as sticky juice dribbles out of your knob and leaks down the inside of my leg. I can see every inch of my cock jamming into you while I'm pushing your ass aggressively up then slamming back down on top of me, reminding you exactly how to ride eight-plus thick inches of meat.

BENCH PLAYER

Taking you over to one of the benches, I sit up with my legs straight out in front of me, and have you sit back on top, your legs straddling me you're bending over till your face is at my feet. I want to feel you breathing heavily on my toes, while you use your legs to rock your ass hard, up and down and back to front, squirming my cock around inside you in every direction. You continue to tease my throbbing knob with your ass, still so tight I could swear it's your first time. It's driving me crazy, watching you slide up and down my glistening pole, as I run my hands down your sweat-covered back and push you further down.

Great view from behind +
feet from the front!

Penetration: deep
Difficulty: medium

LAY UP

I sit up and flip you over the bench, kneel in-between your legs and spread them wide, holding you up by your waist. I sink myself into you as I tear you apart, hearing your short, deep gasping as the blood to rushes to your head. In rhythm with your gasps, I slam into you, my balls slapping loud against you. I can control how wide your legs are, and the wider apart I push them, the deeper I feel myself entering you. I'm brutal with my thrusts, and you are getting off so much on being owned like this, it's not long until loads of cum start to run down your chest from your thick cut cock. I reach over you and rub it all the way down your rock hard teenage abs, before forcing my hands up to your mouth so I can watch you eat it.

Guy on top controls thrust and holds his playmate's waist up
Bottom keeps his body angled up

Penetration: deep
(when you find the right angle)
Difficulty: medium

SLAM DUNK

With your mouth now sticky and wet, you pull yourself up and lean into me, pressing your mouth against mine. I can taste the salty juice I just rubbed all over you, and I can smell it on your breath—intoxicating! I guess there's just one thing left for me to do. I roll you upside down into a ball, making you lick your own low hanging knob while I tear into you from above and teach you the true meaning of dunking. I balance myself on your hole and swish your ass, fucking your brains out. I'm jammed in so far, I feel my knob suddenly expand until it bursts, spilling bucket-loads into you, filling you up so much I can feel you suddenly choking. I think I just made you swallow your own cock and the second load that came with it.

A balancing act - for the experienced only!!
Stretch properly + use core strength for support

Penetration: deep
Difficulty: hard

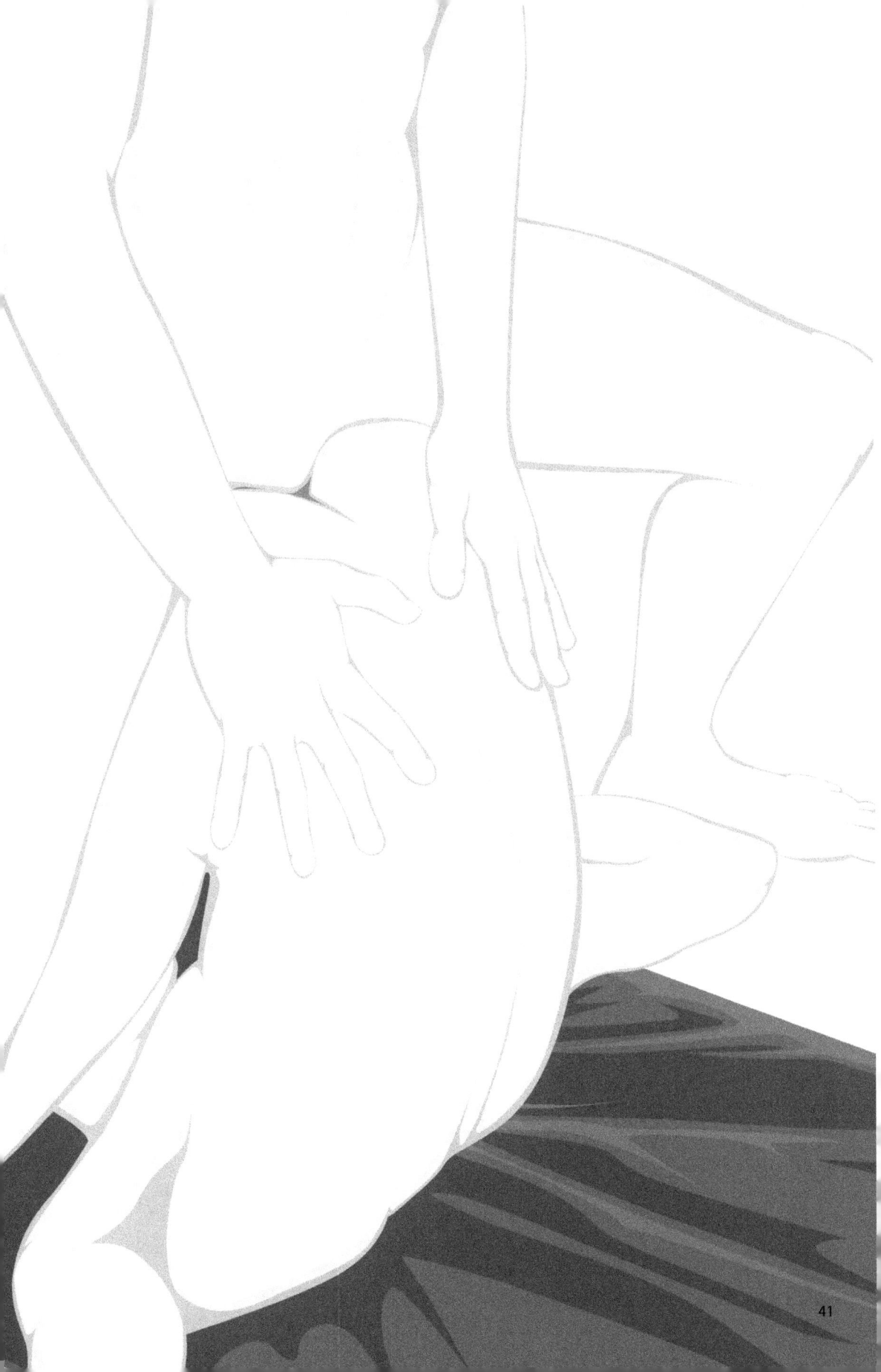

41

1000 Wetsuits Later:

So
let's talk
about the 1000
wetsuits that I've
swum around in. And by
wetsuits I mean condoms
and yes I've used over a
thousand of them. Get the
message yet? I have a lot of
sex and I know my stuff.
I practice safe sex.
Unsafe sex can
fuck you up.

It's as simple as that. Now, my collection of Starting Positions tells a completely different story, but there's a perfectly simple explanation. I had a lot of sex and spent years fucking my playmate's brains out in every filthy way imaginable and then some more you wouldn't even dream of. Pay attention to my careful reference to "playmate" here – I always keep my playmates on a tight leash, and you should learn to do the same. So to clarify, the feeling of bare skin against bare skin is fucking hot and I enjoy every second of it. But the difference between a regular playmate and random sex could not be more simple, and it's important that every one of you get that into those thick heads of yours. While, of course, there can never be a completely fail-safe level of safety associated with an open sexual relationship that involves bare sex, the risk you are taking is trusting in your playmate. It's a two-way street, and the rules are straightforward – you always get regular tests done, and you always SUIT UP WITH A STRANGER. It's a simple game of one strike, you're out. That goes for both of you.

These rules are not meant to be broken, and there are certain rules I always play by, despite a deep seeded enjoyment in breaking every other one I can wrap my hands around. All I can say is that you should use every sweat-dripping and sand-covered thrust of mine as inspiration and learn to play ball as hard as I do. But playing safe does not have to make it any less sexy. Ultra-thin condoms actually feel really hot over the top of my hard cock, and 'double bagging', so placing a second ultra-thin condom over the top of the first one can provide such intense stimulation, you will wonder why the hell you haven't been trying it earlier. DON'T THROW IT AWAY for someone who won't even know your name the morning after.

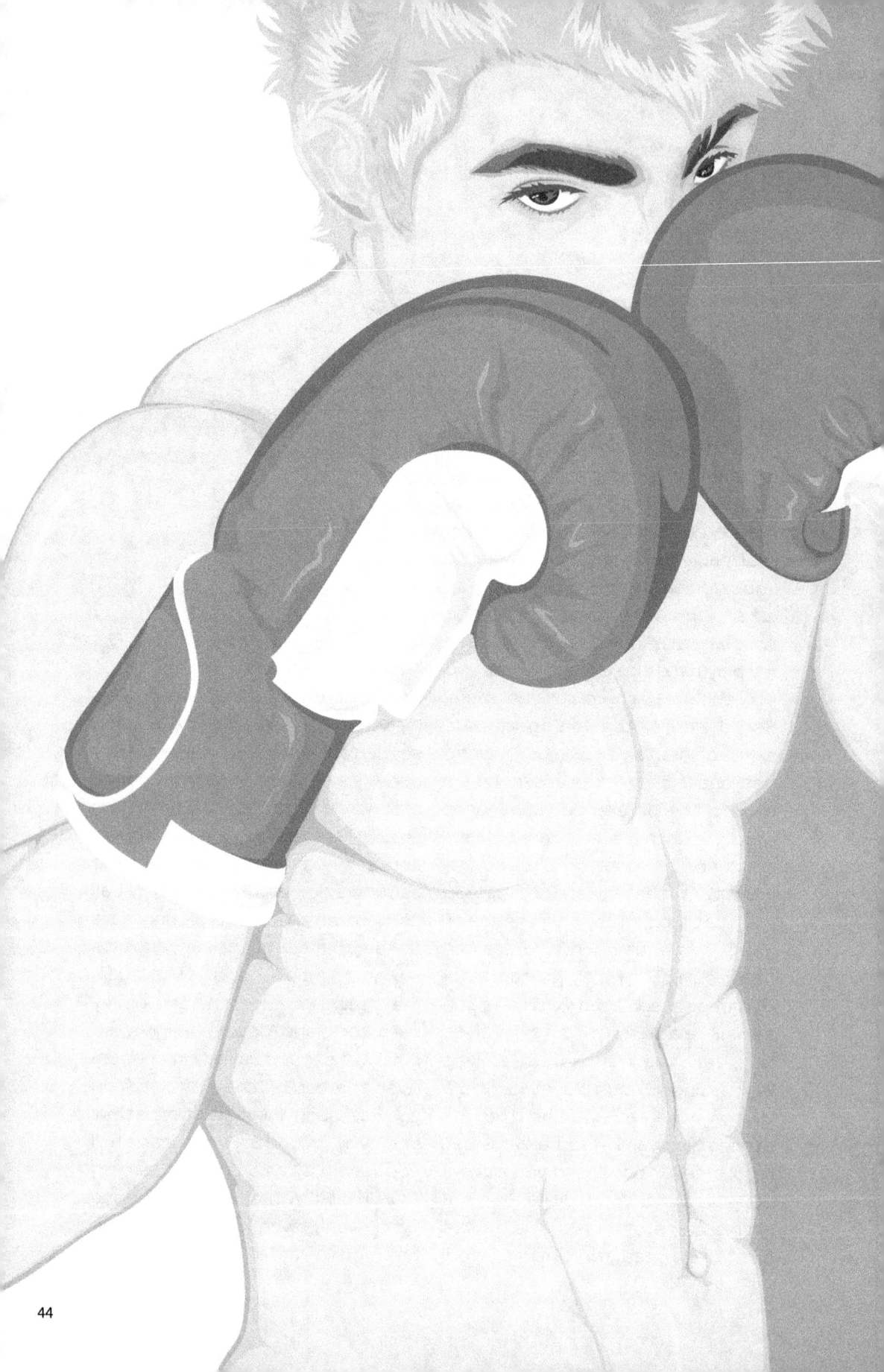

CHAPTER 3

BOXING

Wii boxing was a great way to keep fit. I loved spending afternoons in your living room, knocking each other out. You always insisted on playing shirtless, sporting a pair of baggy cargo shorts that rode low on your ass. After two hours of watching you beat the crap out of me, I was thirsty for the sweat dripping down every part of you. All I wanted was to knock you to the mat and pound the hell out of you.

With your pants that low, your thin, short boxers didn't leave much to the imagination. I could see up one side of them and noticed your thick knob hanging down against the side of your leg. I always found it hard to tell whether your swollen head is hard or soft and its always visible through whatever pants or shorts you're wearing. By this point I've got only one thing on my mind. You're going to get slammed around every corner of the room, like a boxer getting his face pounded in the ring.

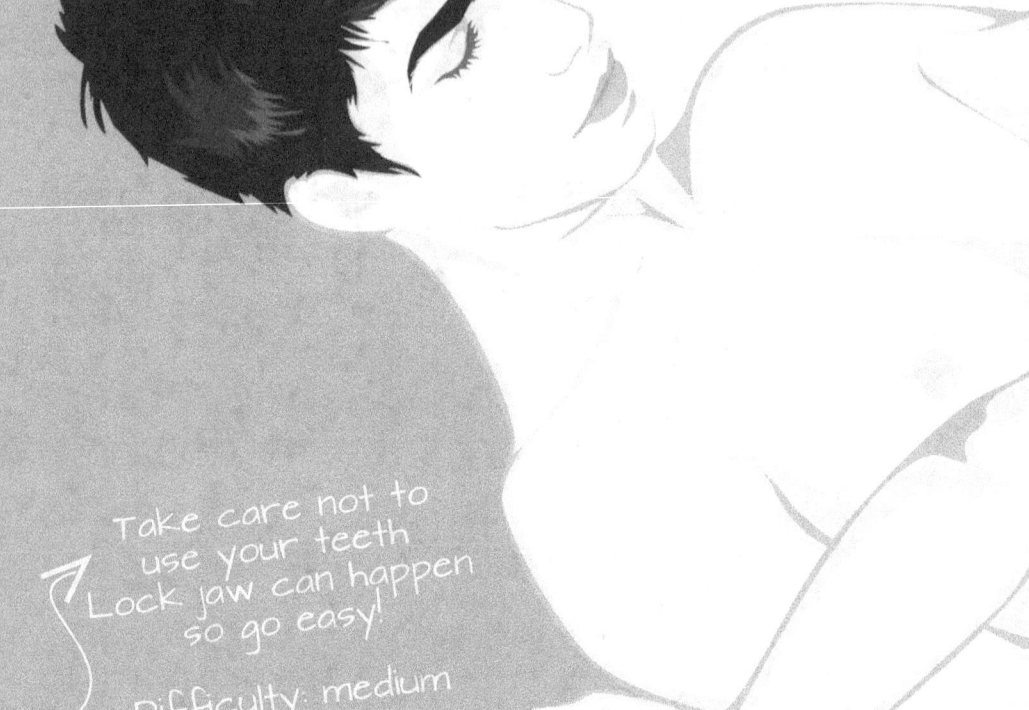

Take care not to use your teeth Lock jaw can happen so go easy!

Difficulty: medium

SCORING BLOW

I reach over, pull your cock out of the side of your shorts, and instantly wrap my lips around it. You aren't fully hard yet, giving me a few seconds to feel that thing growing in my mouth, my moistened lips wrapped around it. As I slide my tongue around, wildly licking your rapidly growing inches, I feel your hand press the back of my head, forcing me to swallow you down to the base. The musky smell of your wet skin and the taste of your sweaty meat make me drool, lubing your pole quickly and making it easy to slide down the back of my throat. You thrust up and into my mouth as I run my hand along your balls, cupping them, rolling them in my palm and sliding my fingers deeper between your legs.

BELOW THE BELT

By now I've worked up quite the appetite for finger fucking you. I move to one of the sofas, where I can sit back and forcefully guide you onto all fours, while making you spread your legs wide. I push your cheeks apart with both hands and stare straight in between your legs. My pole is pressing against your ass, already moistening itself as I start to tease you with the tips of my fingers, spitting on your hole as I work them into you. Using fingers from both hands I stroke my way deeper inside, making sure I'm breaking you in well and feeling you squirm, moaning at how deep my fingers are sliding into you.

Finger foreplay with a view
use fingers + hands to
completely work that ass!

Difficulty: easy

**Cut your fucking nails

CORNER POST

My cock begins to drool sticky pre-cum onto the tight rim of your ass, lubing you up for what's next. I flip you over and pick you up, sliding you down on top of me. I grip your slim, muscular thighs and force your legs into the air until they're balanced over my shoulders. I pull you your ass down onto me, feeling my thick inches force your ass open as I slide into you. When I'm nearly all the way in, I really go for it and pull you down hard, forcing the last inch to jam sharply inside you. My balls slap against your sweat covered skin and your eyes roll back as if you've been hit with a knockout punch. I grip your hips and hold you in position, making sure you keep my throbbing knob firmly in place, while your own swollen cock bounces around and jabs me in the stomach.

I love the feeling of my cock grinding slowly inside you, especially with you sitting on top of me. Over and over my tight skin rubs back and forth within the depths of your bare hole, making me want to give up all control and just pummel you as hard as I can.

Team effort all the way but totally worth the result!
Penetration: deep
Difficulty: hard

Hands can do some serious spreading = intense penetration!

Difficulty: easy

JAB

You pretend to act surprised as I throw you up against the table, bend you over and spread your ass cheeks apart so I can get right in between your legs. Well, pretty boy, there's nothing surprising about what's coming next. I slam into you relentlessly, holding nothing back, your knuckles turning white as you try to hold on and take it all. The hard thrusts of my thick inches push your cheeks further apart as I force deeper into you, giving you no choice but to just stand there and take every inch I give you.

TOE TO TOE

I slam you face down on the floor and get on top of you. I'm in the mood to run my tongue down the soles of your smooth boy feet as I try to insert myself even further into you. Upside down, I force my hot, rigid cock inside you until I feel your smooth ass tense around my cock so tightly that I can barely push any further. Cock deep inside you, my thick inches begin to chafe the inside of your hole. I can't possibly get any deeper, and you're gasping so hard now it seems like I've really abused the hell out of you. Just like I intended.

Getting the angle right is key to achieving maximum enjoyment!
++ Feet play

Penetration: deep
Difficulty: hard

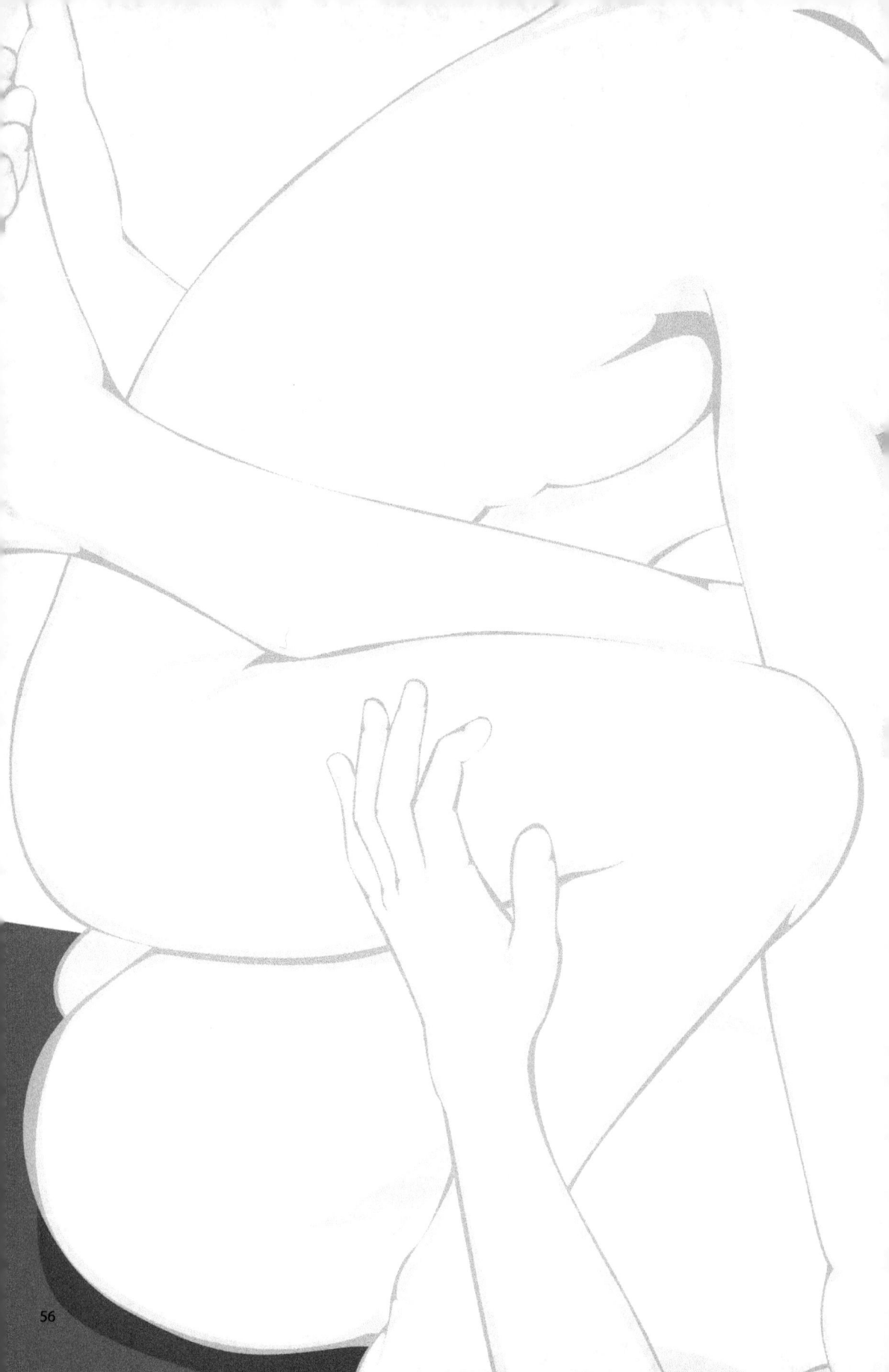

CLINCH

I want to be sure you remember for days to come what it feels like to have my cock jammed that far in you. So now I let you take control of having your own ass ripped apart. Clinch down on top of me, bitch, so I can do the last bit of damage needed to finish you off. As you rock back and forth on top of me, obediently taking every inch just the way I like, I feel my balls ready to burst their thick load. Reacting instantly, you reach down and eagerly stroke the top of your knob. Within seconds, your cock explodes hard, shooting me square in the face and drenching me in a thick shower of your sticky mess. I respond by pouring my hot load into your ass, until it's running out the sides of your hole. You have made such a filthy mess, I'm forced to grab you by the hair and make you get down on your knees in front of me and use your tongue to lick up every last bit. Get down there and polish my softening cock until it's clean again.

Not a position for the amateur + serious teamwork involved!

Penetration: deep
Difficulty: hard

CHAPTER 4

CRICKET

Rain breaks during summer holiday cricket games were a hell of a lot of fun. Australian summers usually called for rain, which in turn involved spending more time playing with another kind of bat and ball. We usually played small backyard games or jumped the fence of one of the local cricket pitches. There was always an empty change room around the back of the pitch, which is where you would take most of your fastballs every time it started to rain. Escaping from the rain into the change rooms, we were always dripping wet and covered in mud, both eager to strip off and hit the showers for a good soaping down.

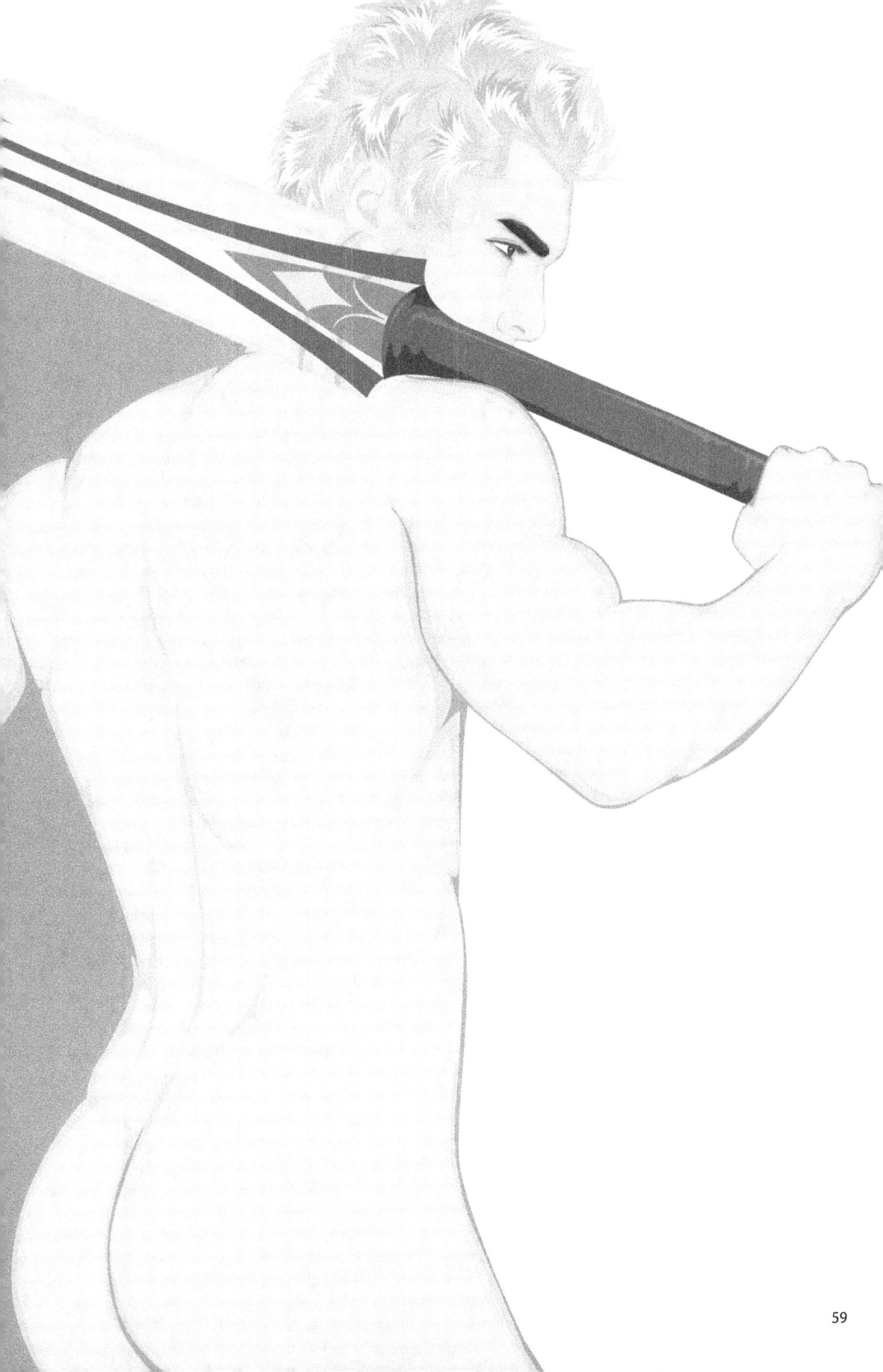

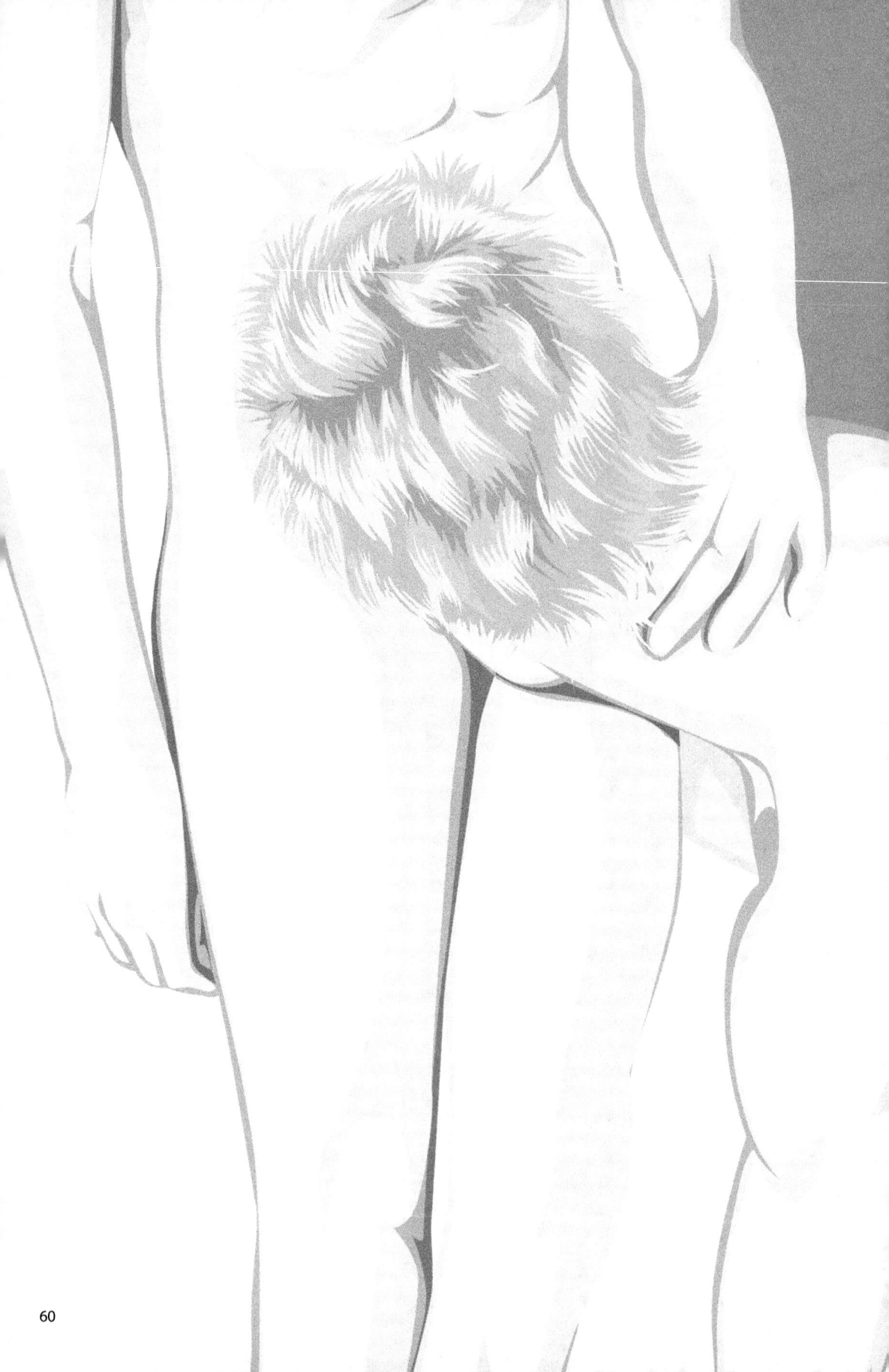

MIDDLE STUMP

would start by soaping you from head to toe, rubbing your lean teenage body under the running water and slowly working my way down toward your throbbing slab of meat. It wasn't long until I was down on my knees in front of you, wrapping my lips around your thick knob and running my tongue over your long, hard inches. The water under the showers was only ever lukewarm at best, so your balls were always bunched up and nut full, making them so much fun to play with. Down on my knees, I submitted as you grabbed the back of my head and smacked me in the face, then shoved your teenage bat down my throat.

Recommended usage: daily - anywhere, anytime

Difficulty: easy

Backward push ups
+ extreme teamwork needed!

Penetration: deep
Difficulty: medium

BACK LIFT

You had a horny gleam in your eye, and I knew what was coming next. This teenager was about to get his revenge. Throwing me back so I was leaning up on my hands and feet, you quickly slid between my legs and started to soap me up on the tiled shower floor. Your fingers roughly slid in between my spread cheeks, while you rubbed your throbbing head with your other hand, soaping it up and getting ready to punish me with it. Without warning, you plunged into me and didn't hesitate for a second until you were balls deep inside me. You spread my legs wide and took to my ass like an energizer bunny, breathing heavily and making sure I felt each deliberate thrust penetrate my insides the same way I had torn yours apart on so many occasions. I reared up and suddenly felt your teenage enthusiasm busting inside me, filling me with your warm load.

LEG BREAK

Now it's your turn to get punished. Still recovering from your cock, I aggressively throw you onto your back and stretch your legs apart, pulling your left leg up over my shoulder so I can spread you as wide as possible. I soap up your ass and ram two fingers into you hard, just to remind you who's boss. You let out a gasp, then a pleased moan, impressed with how hard my uncut cock is as you wrap your hand around it, eagerly anticipating having every inch inside you. I rub some soap up and down my solid knob and jam my throbbing head into you. It takes just seconds to slide all the way inside and penetrate you to the core.

Lean in to find the right balance + use leg in the air for support

Penetration: controlled
Difficulty: medium

ROUND THE WICKET

'm back in control and you like it this way. You roll over onto your side, keeping me tightly squeezed inside you. With one leg up over my shoulder, your ass is completely spread, giving me full access to your begging hole. I continue to slam you, sliding my soaped up fingers in between your toes so I can hold your leg right where it is and keep you open as wide as I want. Your moans grow louder and longer, the harder I go. I use one hand to grab your cheek, stretching you open further as I slide in a finger, your tight hole agape as I continue to slam you.

Sideways penetration is usually intense and can be deep, but controlled

Difficulty: Hard

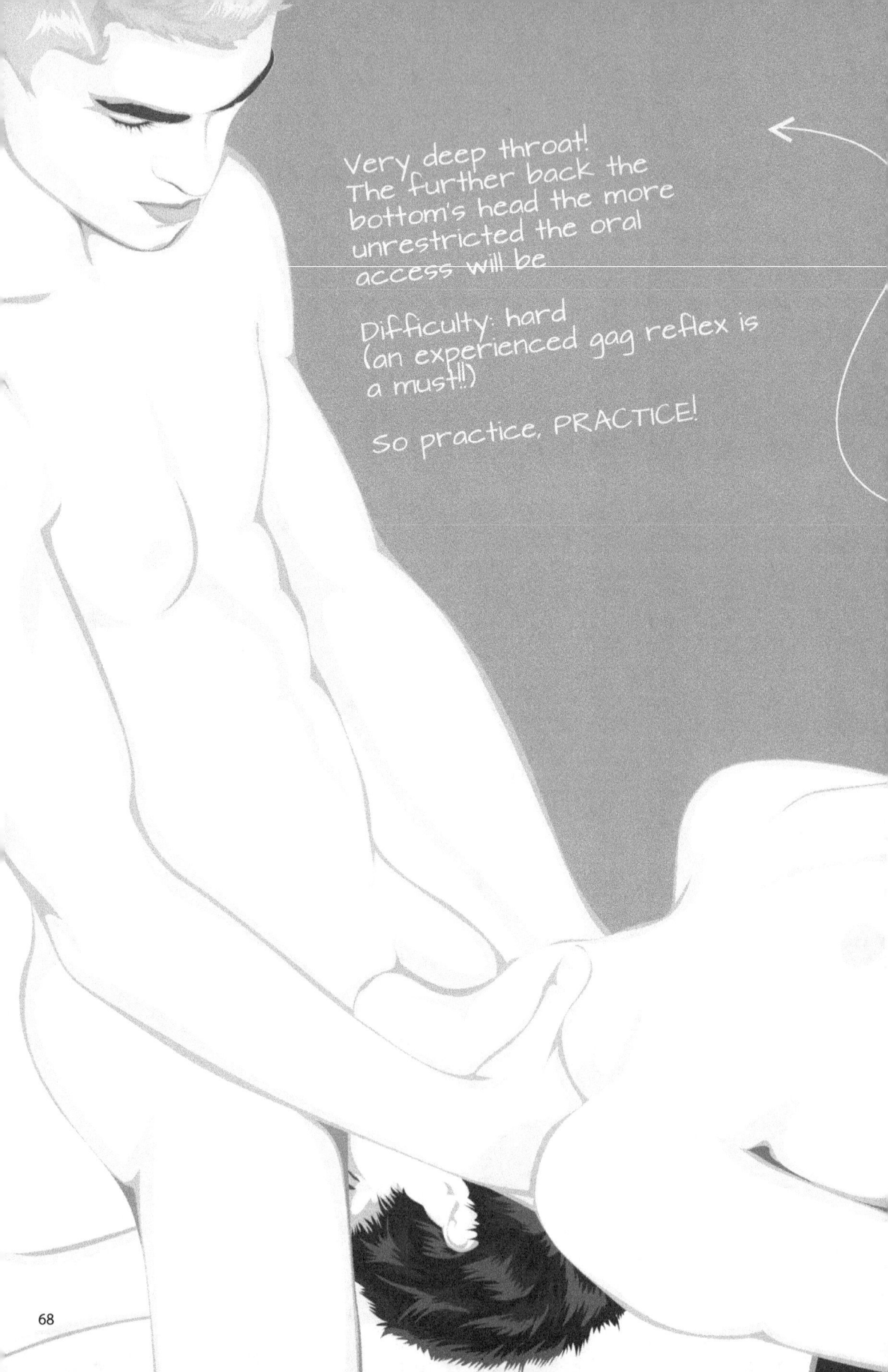

Very deep throat!
The further back the
bottom's head the more
unrestricted the oral
access will be

Difficulty: hard
(an experienced gag reflex is
a must!!)

So practice, PRACTICE!

FRENCH CUT

The combination of my finger and my cock makes it so tight in there that I'm ready to blow my first load, and your throat is where it's heading. I throw you up onto one of the benches so your head is hanging over the edge, and I kneel right up beside it. I grab you by the face and force every one of my inches deep into your throat, fucking your face as aggressively as you can take it. My hands wrap around your throat and feel you gagging as I choke you with my thick meat. My body shudders as my thick load begins to shoot down the back of your throat. Your moan muffled by the sheer amount of what I've just dumped in there.

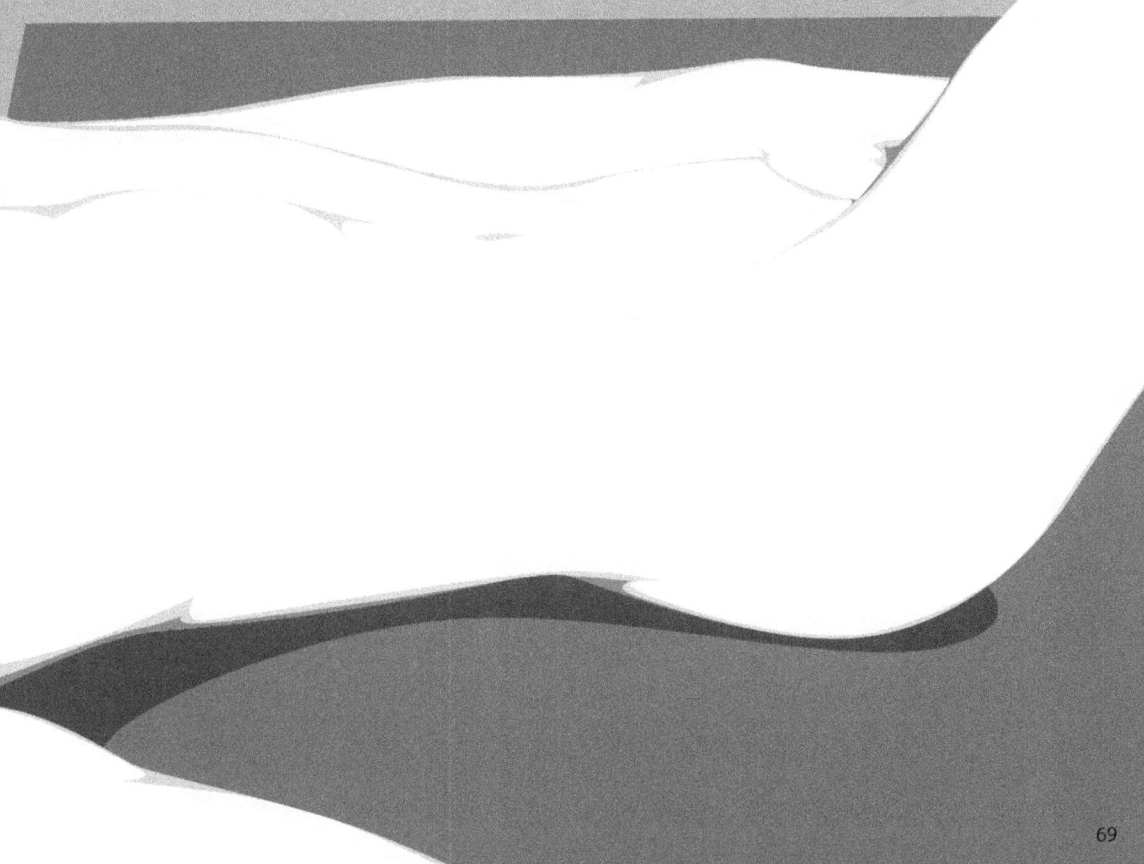

LEG STUMP

My fingers find their way into you again, and your hole is practically begging for me to pound it some more, after filling your face the way I just did. Get up on top of me, teenager; this inning isn't over. I lie down on the bench and spread my legs wide enough to allow you to slide down on top of me. Grabbing hold of your body, I make you take every inch again and again; as I lie there and watch you ride me hard. I fill your tight, puckered hole with everything I've got, using my hands to open you a bit wider, so I can get in that little bit deeper.

Using the top's knees for support penetration can be steady and controlled

Penetration: deep
Difficulty: medium

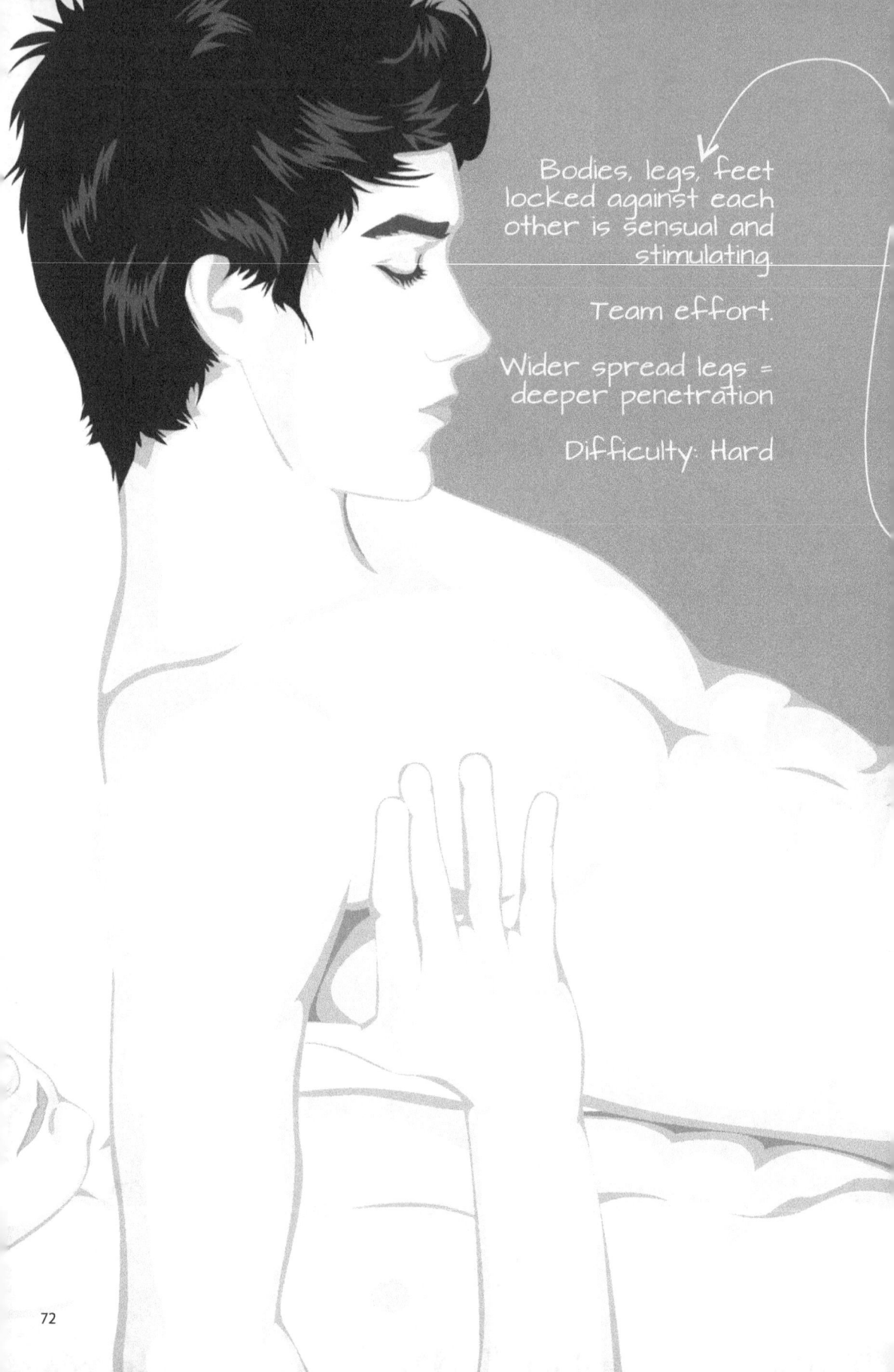

Bodies, legs, feet locked against each other is sensual and stimulating.

Team effort.

Wider spread legs = deeper penetration

Difficulty: Hard

LOFTED DRIVE

Your ass is so smooth, hot and tight that I have to blow my load again. You have taken my cock so deep and hard that I can already feel the second load is going to be as big as the first. Grabbing you from behind and forcing you down on top of me, I make you feel each last penetrating blow. You pin me down, your body slamming against mine, until that teenage ass milks every last drop out of me. Finally I let my flaccid cock slip out of you, tingling, turn you to face me and press my exhausted body against yours. I lead you back into the shower to soap up again and wash down. I've used you well and look forward to our next match.

SEX in five 5 BASES

Kissing

»

Jerking

»

Oral & Rimming

Fingering

Fucking

CHAPTER 5

DIVING

Naked bomb dives into the pool during summer were by far the best use of a diving board I could ever imagine. Watching you do flips and twist your body into all sorts of revealing angles made me want to twist you into completely filthy angles myself. Of course, you wore a pair of tiny black Speedos, which I made sure never stayed on for very long. Bent over the diving board, you knew how to tease, baring a glimpse of your smooth, tight ass before plunging into the water. Knowing exactly how to respond, I would dive in straight after you and hold you under the water, forcing you into some back flips of my own.

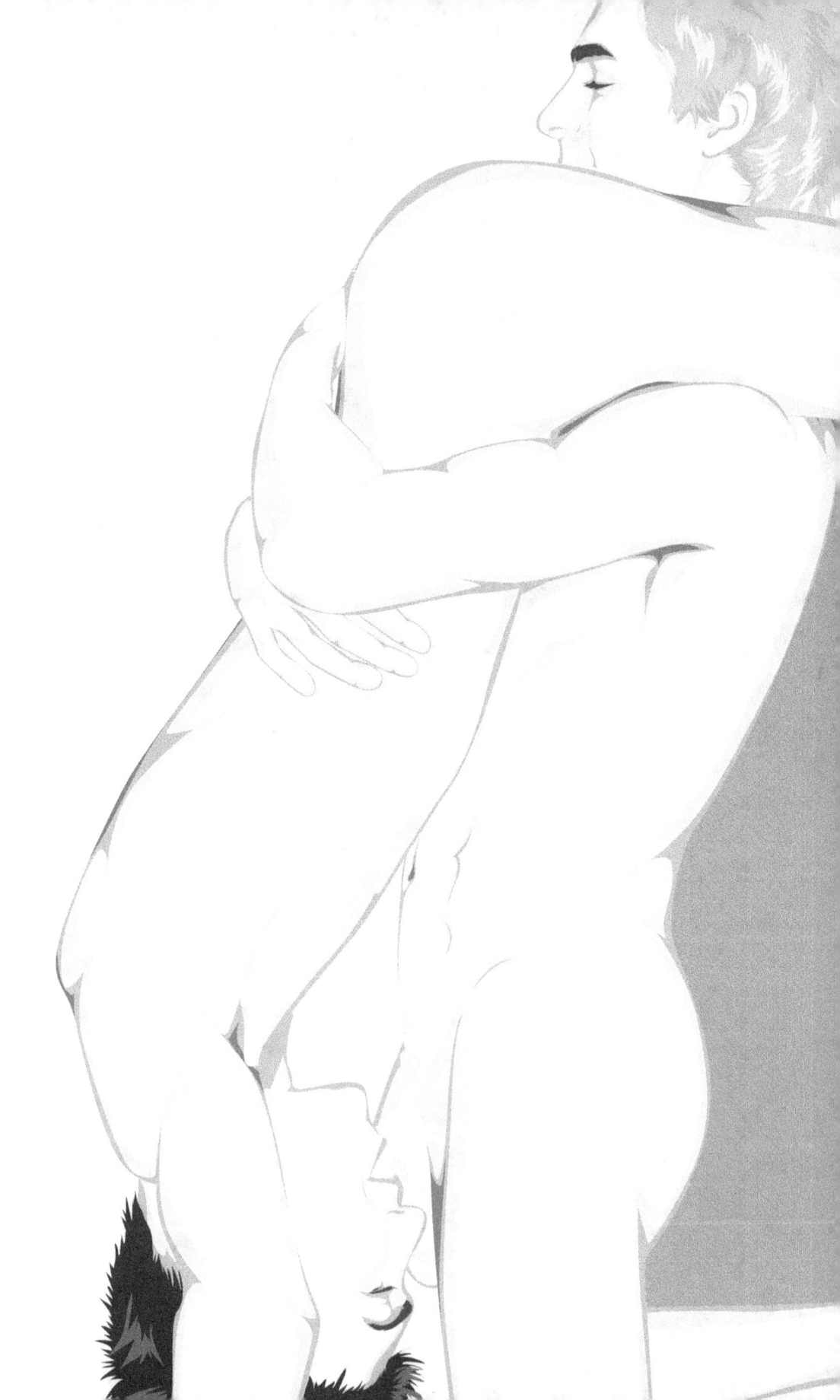

HANDSTAND

In the water, the weightlessness of your body lets me have some serious fun with you. Swimming around and thrashing wildly, my hands find their way in between your legs. I pull your ass up to my face and hold you upside down, so you can cop a face-full of your own. You've teased me long enough, so I aggressively tongue you, giving your little butt the attention it deserves.

I feel your lips wrap around my foreskin and take me as far into your mouth as you want. I'm beyond rock hard right now, completely turned on by eating you out, and I can feel myself moistening down the back of your throat as

Mutual mouthfuls, up-side-down!

Difficulty: hard

PLUNGE DIVE

Finally surfacing, you gasp for air and wait for me to make my next move. Leading you over to the side of the pool, I help you discover that there's an even better use for your diving board. Standing behind you, I run my hands down your back and grab onto your firm cheeks, giving you a taste of what's to come as I slowly slide two fingers into you. Putting your leg up next to mine, you arch your back and push your ass further toward me, wanting more. I grab my cock with one hand, and force it inside you. You let out a deep moan as I remind you exactly how big I am, and how keen my hard cock is to get into you.

Great everyday position + normal 'beginners' penetration achieved

Penetration: medium
Difficulty: easy

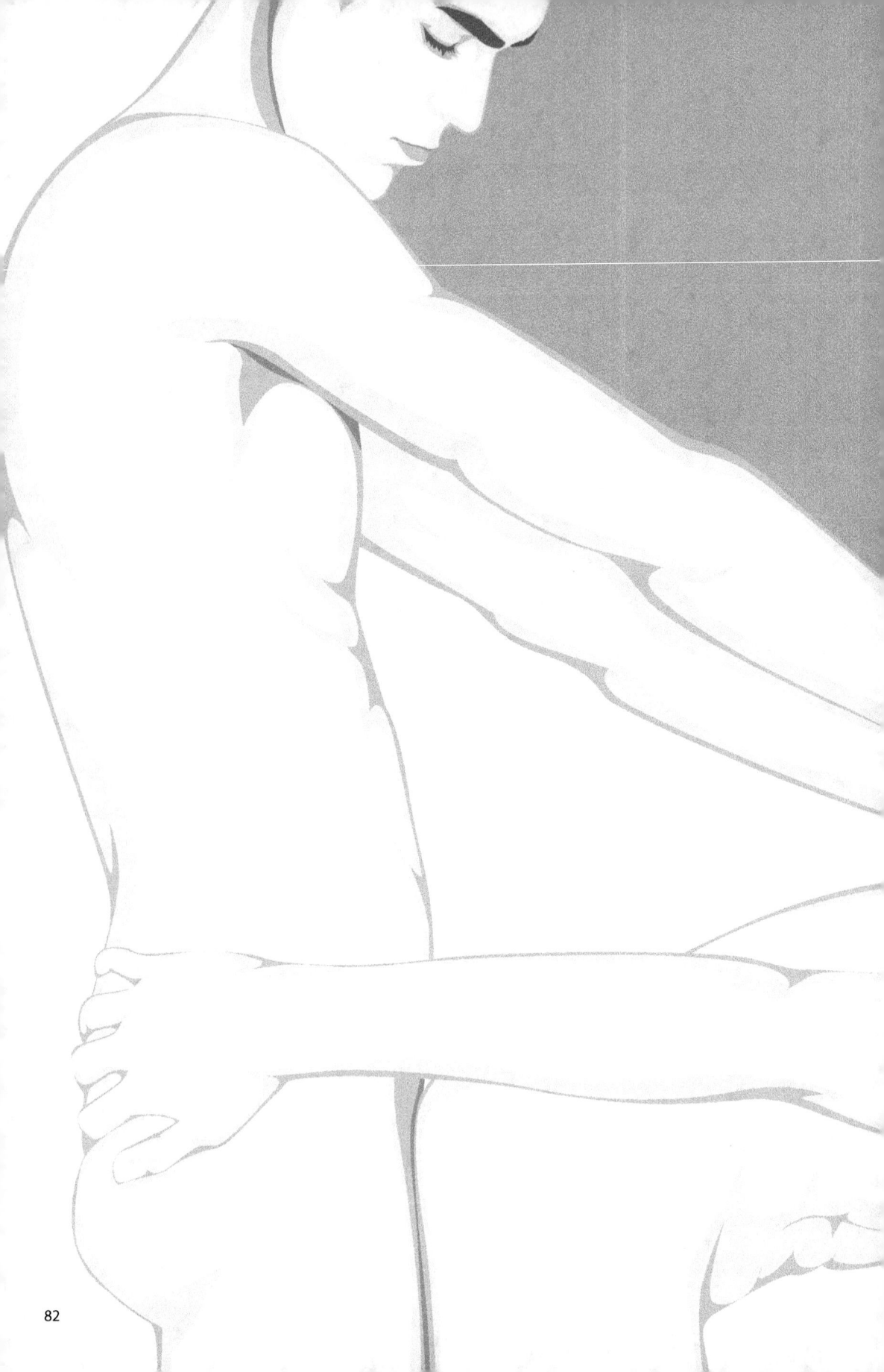

OPEN PIKE

Bending yourself in half for a one-and-a-half pike is so much better served impaled on my inches than wasted on a diving board. Your long legs look stunning from behind, and bent at the waist your ass pouts straight out at me, inviting me to dive in-throbbing "head" first. Holding you by the shoulders and forcing myself all the way in, you grab my hips and pull me in even further. You're begging for it now, and I'm more than willing to oblige with everything I've got. The direct intensity I deliver from where I'm standing satisfies every part of your now-violently shaking body, and in a matter of seven heightened minutes, those years of practicing on the diving team just paid off. I splash a perfect "10" deep up in you, and listen to your satisfied moans.

Arm strength + balance are key to
achieving greater depth
Pull hard from above
and below

Penetration: deep
Difficulty: medium

TUCK

Cum still leaking out of your punished hole, I throw you over my shoulder and dive back into the pool, twisting you as you smack hard into the water. Spotting the stairs in the corner of the pool, we swim over to the edge, where I tuck your legs underneath you to make your little ass oblige by pushing out towards me. Perfect working height from where I'm standing. Holding onto your waist, I have plenty of leverage to drill you deep and hard. Your ass feels so tight up against my pole that it simply deserves to be bent over in the pool all summer long. My big balls slap against you loudly as I thrust, exciting you to moan louder and louder with each smack, which only makes me pound you harder. The water splashes violently all around, showering us as you beg for more, immensely turned on as I run my hands up and down your smooth, wet skin.

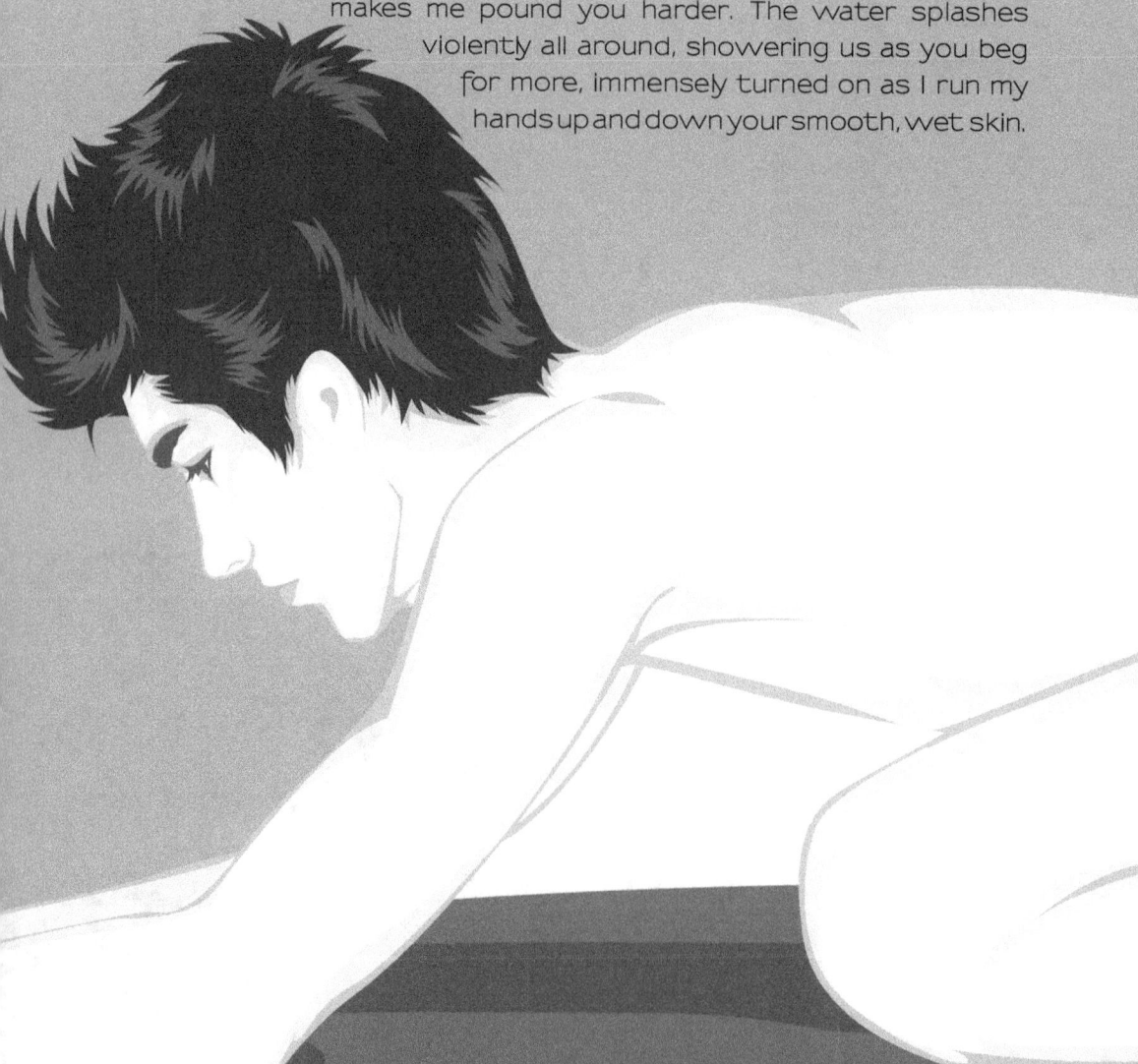

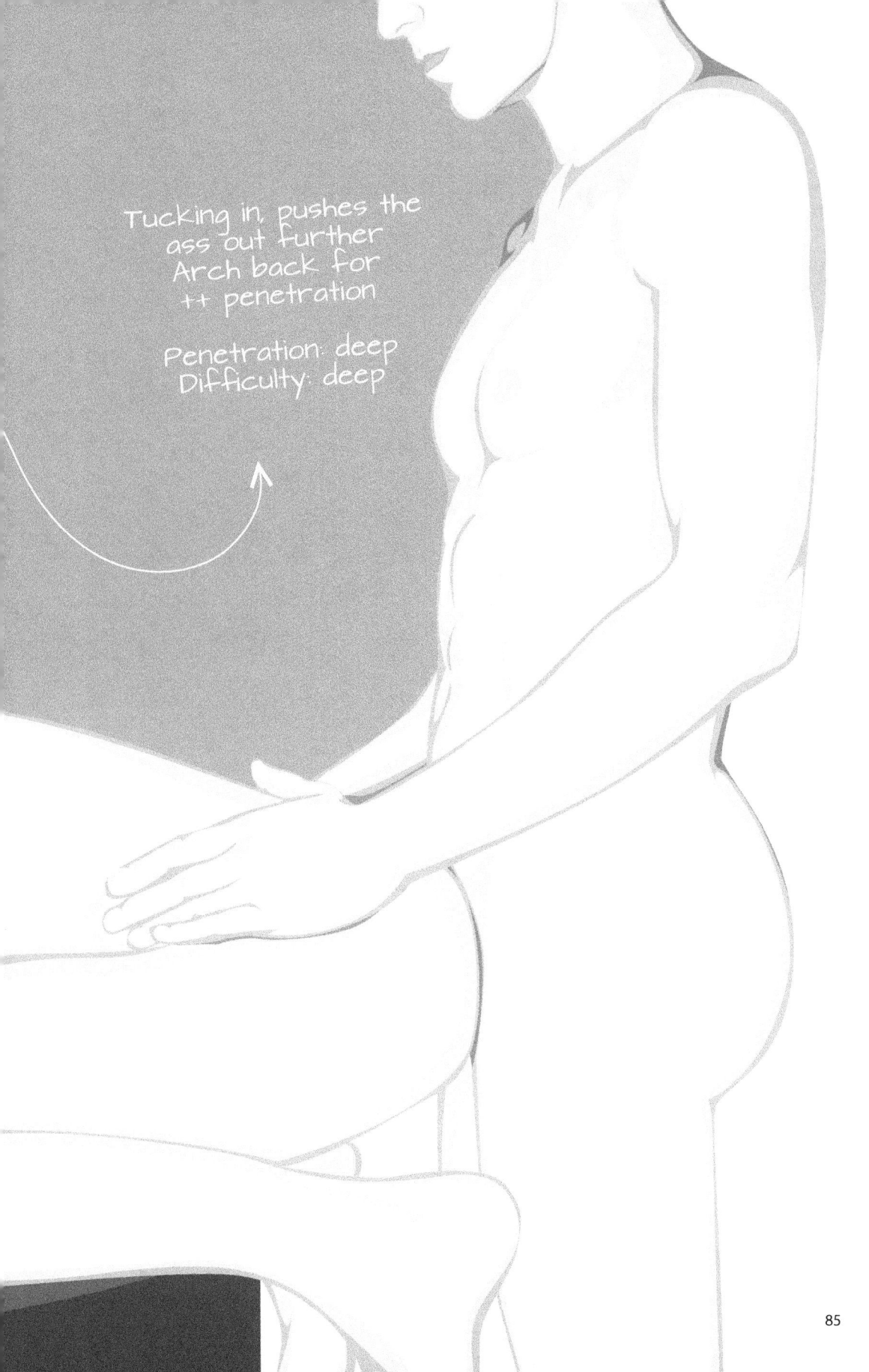

Tucking in, pushes the
ass out further
Arch back for
++ penetration

Penetration: deep
Difficulty: deep

Balancing and some
furniture needed!
Penetration : medium
Difficulty : hard

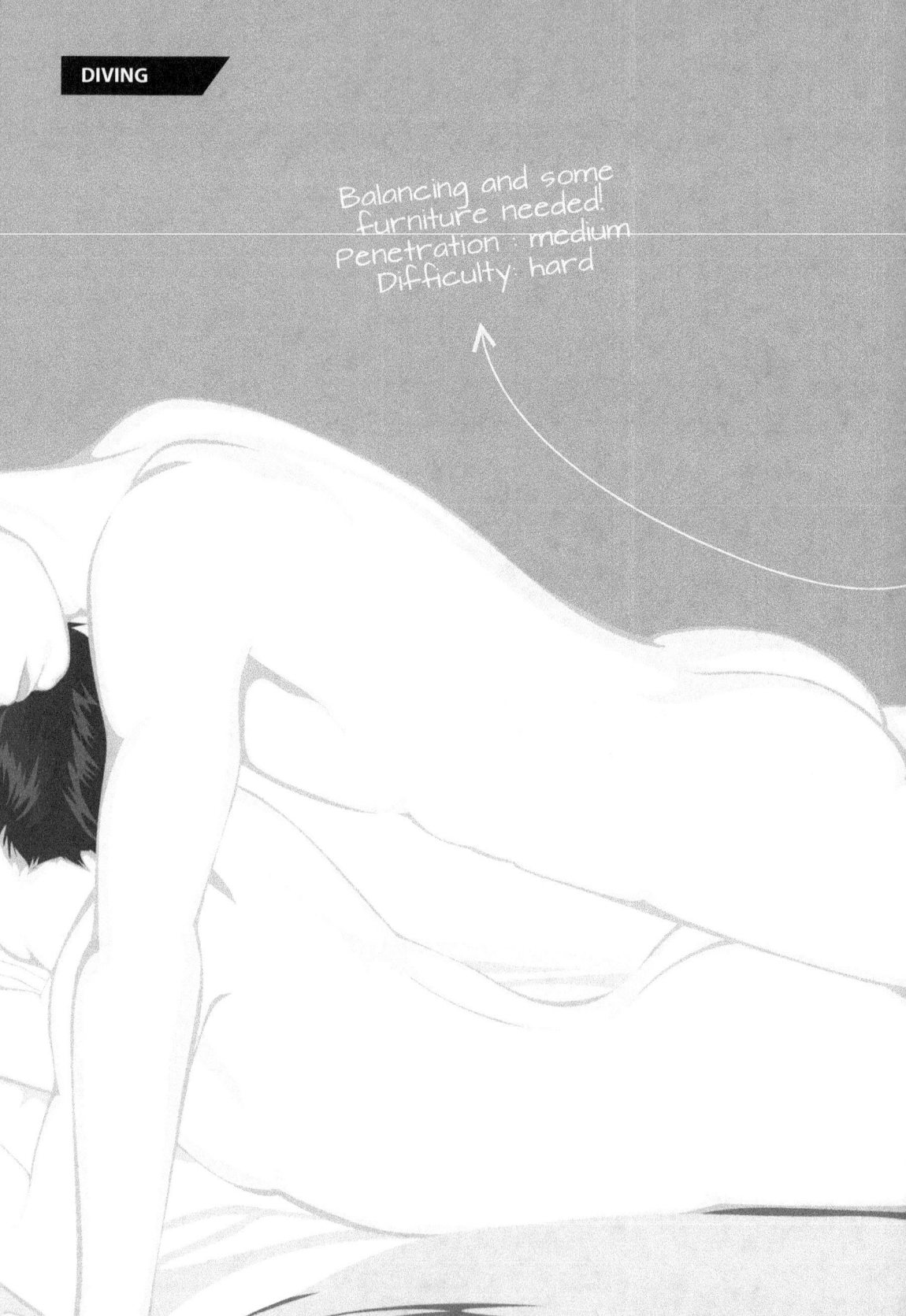

ARMSTAND DIVE

Leading you out of the pool and over to the daybed, I lay you facedown and use the ledge to prop my legs, so I can forcefully and deliberately push into you from above. I tell you to start counting backwards from a hundred, and with each number of your count I sink down into you, pushing back up for the next one. Each time I pull my hard, wet cock out just far enough to leave my throbbing head still in, then force it all the way back in each time. The slamming gets faster as you hit the twenties and then the teens, and by the time you reach zero, you tell me to just sit there inside you, and I feel your hole tensing around my cock as you let out a loud moan and start to blow all over the bed, launching a sticky mess all up your stomach.

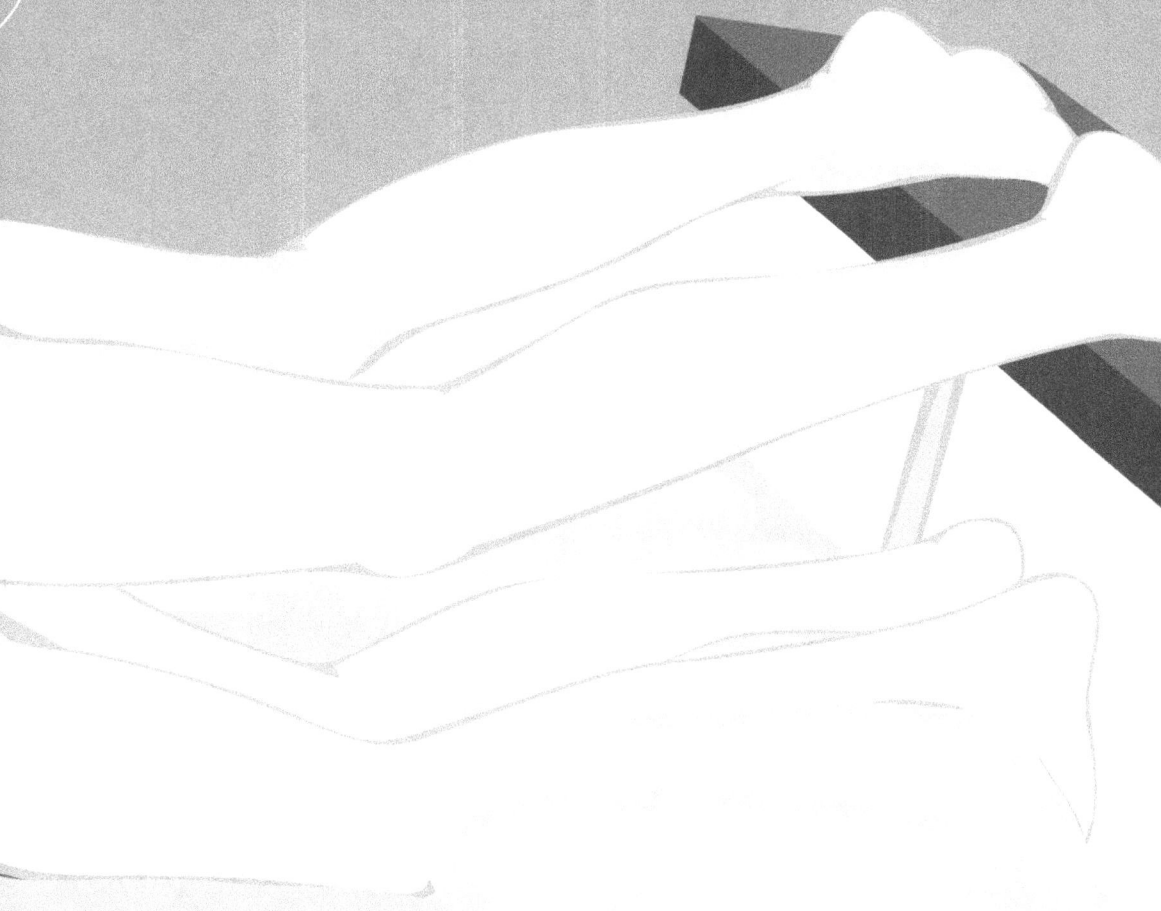

BACKWARD DIVE

The intensity of your moan has just made me want to fill your teenage hole even more. You use the ledge to hold yourself up, and I watch you slide your half flaccid cut cock up against your lips, as I slide mine back into you. I'm so deep inside you now, your moans stop, and I hear you sucking on your own cock. That's all the reason I need to let my load go. I push into you one last time, enough to feel your ass swallow my huge load, and bust my nut just as you're choking down a second load of your own, your ass tensing around my inches in rhythm with my spasms. That seriously has to be one of your hottest sex tricks! And I know I'm going to enjoy this summer immensely!

Experience + total body co-ordination is a must. Totally sexy results!

Penetration: (very) deep
Difficulty: hard

CHAPTER 6

FOOTBALL

You caught my attention during practice one night. There's just something about long soccer socks wrapped half way up your smooth teenage legs that really turns me on. I wink at you as I think of all the filthy things I want to do to you on the field. You hang around until it's just the two of us left kicking the soccer ball around in our loose soccer shorts. I can tell you're not wearing anything underneath them as your big cock flops around, nearly falling out each time you jump from side to side.

You toss your shirt aside, and instantly I feel my cock start to rise in my shorts, watching the sweat glistening off your smooth, athletic teenage chest. I catch you grinning as you stare down at my shorts and notice the outline of my hardening bulge through the thin layer of nylon, begging to get out. It's time to wipe that smirk off your face.

Kicking the ball in your direction, I throw myself after it, tackling you to the ground until I'm sitting on top of your chest, pinning you down. There's mud on your face as you look up at me with a cheeky grin, waiting for me to take control. You have no idea...

Foreplay (rimming)
Use hands to
spread cheeks apart

Difficulty: easy!

GOAL MOUTH

I can feel you breathing rapidly as my hands explore your toned, sweat covered body. In a swift move I pull your shorts down to your ankles to reveal your thick nine inches staring me in the face. 'Not bad ey' you grin as you pull my shorts halfway down my ass and plough your face straight in between my sweaty cheeks. I rear up, just enough to feel your wet tongue running down my gooch and starting to tickle my low hanging balls. I'm starting to enjoy this, and I can see from your fast moistening pole that you are too. It's time I take a turn.

BACK TACKLE

Jumping up I order you to get up too. You mutter in agreement with a half-raised eyebrow just in time for me to push you up against the soccer net and get down on my knees behind you. I had been eyeing your toned little ass for the past two hours and could not wait to get my mouth into it. Grabbing your cheeks, I slowly run my tongue up your slightly spread thighs and along your perky little butt, which is begging for attention. I feel you shudder as my tongue starts to circle your hole, tickling you. Your left leg tenses and your toes begin to curl as I rip your cheeks apart with both hands and aggressively start tongue-fucking your hole.

Use your hands + fingers to explore front + back!!

Difficulty: easy

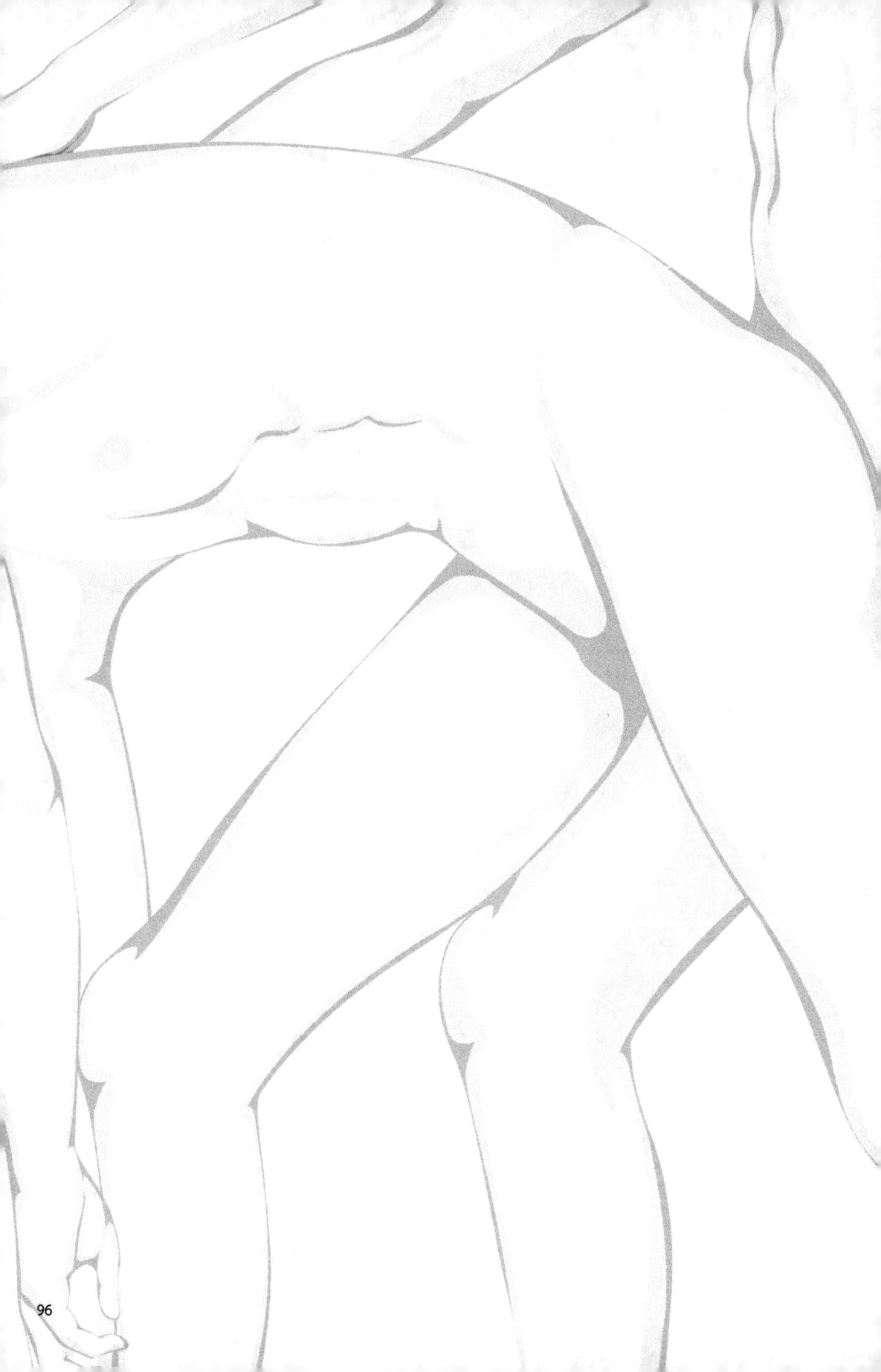

Good, hard thrusts
Perfectly angled to
lean in and go hard

Penetration: deep
Difficulty: easy

DRAG BACK

It doesn't take long for you lean over the edge of the net and bend in half until you're touching your toes. I can feel you run your hand along my hard, dripping cock, telling me that you're ready for it. Immediately I'm standing up behind you and slapping your poised butt with my throbbing pole. It's go time! I grab you by the shoulders and push my cock into you, finding it hard to control myself. You let out a series of gasps, begging me to take it slow as your tight hole wraps itself eagerly around the moist pole sliding in. Your soft moans grow louder the deeper I go. I want to make you feel every inch. Your legs tense up and start to tremble as my pounding gets more ruthless.

CHEST TRAP

My cock still inside you, I force you back down onto the dampening grass. You're on both knees as I wrap my right hand around your throat and pull you back towards me. Your breathing slows a bit, as I'm not as deep as I was before. I want you to relax so I can work my way deeper into you while I pull you back and press your body against mine. With swift, deliberate thrusts, I begin to smash your ass again, making sure you can feel every inch.

Great 'normal' penetration achieved here

Difficulty: easy

HALF BACK

Leaning back, I pull you down so you're sitting on top of me. You place your shaky hands on my knees and start to gently ride up and down on my hard pole. It doesn't take long until I can feel your back arch and you're heaving yourself up and down, getting harder and more intense with each and every thrust. You're riding me so hard you're out of breath, I feel my knob start to tingle. I push you off my cock and pull out, only to have you to grab it tightly and start jerking at it, feeling my pre-cum slowly leaking onto your fingers.

Bottom is on top
Arch back for
deeper penetration

Penetration: deep
Difficulty: easy

THIGH TRAP

You jump on my back and we sprint naked across the field to the change rooms, your hard cock sticky and oozing against my back. We are both covered in mud and sweat, and there's one position I want to throw you in before we jump under the showers together. I lay you flat across the coach's desk, so I can get in between your legs and thrash you from behind. Without warning I take my throbbing inches and jam them straight into you, while standing between your eagerly spread legs. Your muffled moan gets caught in the back of your throat as I get in real deep and hit that spot I know is going to get you off. Seconds later I can feel your cock burst, dripping cum all over my feet, as your hole tenses around my big pole, swallowing it deeper than it's been before. It feels so used and wet in there, all I want to do is finish you off now.

Spread legs wider apart for deeper penetration..

Penetration: deep
Difficulty: medium

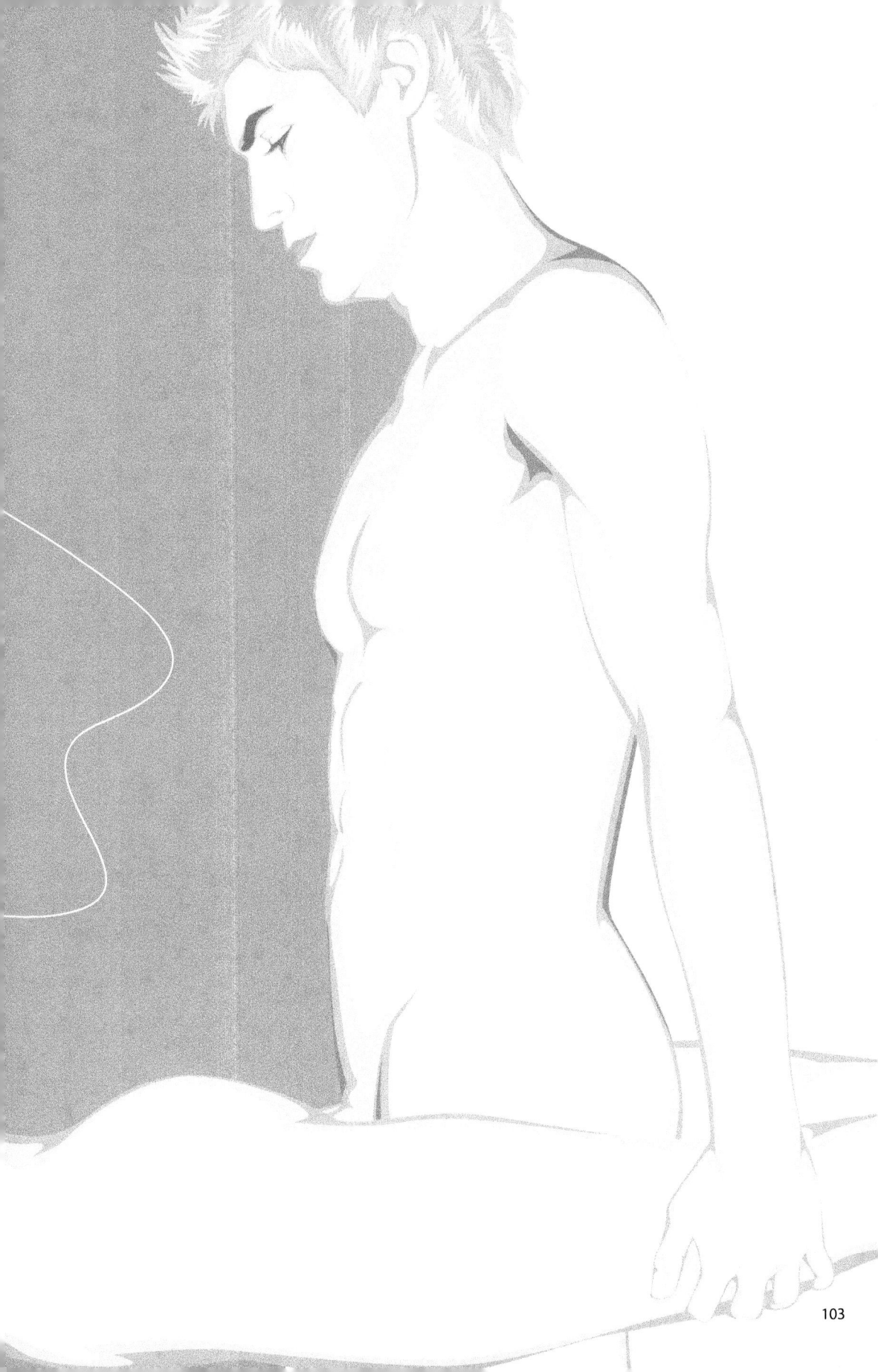

Adjust bodies to
find the right angle.
Might take some
practice.

Penetration:
Deep

MAN TO MAN MARKING

I stand at the edge of the showers watching you rinse your still hard cock and soap up your abused hole. I'm jerking myself slowly as you begin to finger yourself, seeing that it's getting me off. Your eyes roll back as you jam another finger inside, going harder each time you slide your fingers in and out. With my nut ready to burst, I slam you down onto the tiled floor and hammer you from behind, at an angle that lets me slide so deep inside you that your body instantly becomes limp. It only takes a couple of solid thrusts before you feel me spill my massive load into you. Your screams turn into whimpering moans as my thick head explodes, stretching your hole further apart with every throb. Eight bursts later you slump on the floor, completely fucked. You turn your head toward me, just far enough to give me that same little smirk that made me want to rip your soccer shorts off you during training a few hours ago.

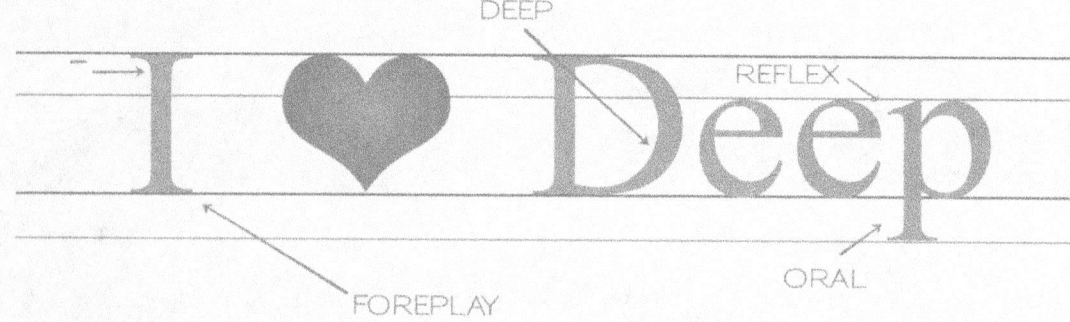

DEEP

REFLEX

FOREPLAY

ORAL

I ♥ Deep

TRY THIS @HOME

AS THE NAME SUGGESTS DEEP-THROATING INVOLVES BASICALLY SWALLOWING YOUR PLAYMATE'S COCK.

IT'S A REALLY DEEP THROAT-PENETRATING BLOWJOB.

NOTES:
PRACTICE MAKES PERFECT: YOU NEED TO CONDITION YOUR GAG REFLEX TO ACCEPT YOUR PLAYMATE'S COCK DOWN THE BACK OF YOUR THROAT.

THIS FOREPLAY TAKES SOME SKILL & IF IT'S YOUR FIRST TIME IT PROBABLY WON'T HAPPEN STRAIGHT AWAY.

TRY PRACTICING AT HOME USING YOUR FINGERS TO START, AND THEN A TOY BEFORE TRYING IT ON YOUR PLAYMATE.

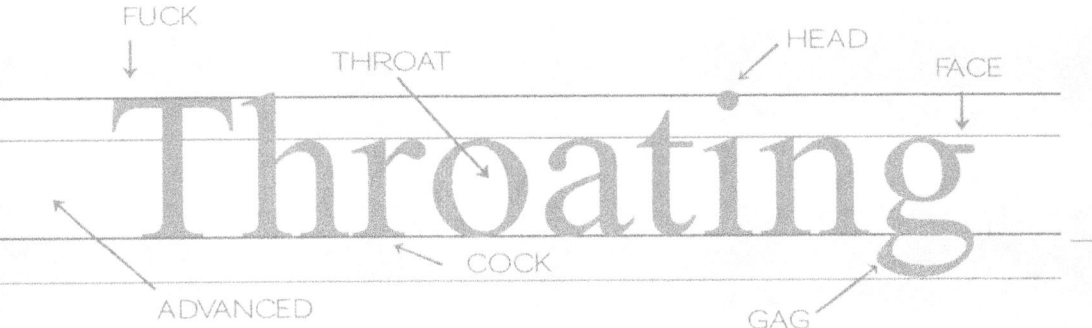

FUCK

THROAT

HEAD

FACE

Throating

COCK

ADVANCED

GAG

BREATHE DEEP AND RELAX WHEN YOU FEEL YOUR GAG REFLEX KICK IN. PULL OUT AS SOON AS IT DOES, WHILE YOU ARE LEARNING TO CONTROL YOUR GAG REFLEX.

IT'S NOT FOR EVERYONE – SOME GUYS HAVE REALLY SENSITIVE GAG REFLEXES AND JUST AREN'T CUT OUT FOR IT. DON'T WORRY TOO MUCH THERE'S PLENTY OF OTHER "SPECIAL SKILLS" TO GET GOOD AT.

I ❤ KOC

CHAPTER 7

GOLF

It's almost as though having the "boy next door" living down the end of my street wasn't enough, but living out on the golf course made for incredible sex on the greens on more than one occasion. You would poke your head through my bedroom window late at night wearing nothing but a short pair of checkered boxer shorts. Inviting me out to play the back nine, your smooth athletic body was almost naked and begging to be thrown around.

That particular night I was lying in bed naked with my hand wrapped around my cock, jerking off, when you caught me in the middle of it. There was no hiding the outline of your big teenage pole instantly hardening as you stood there at my window watching me play with myself. You mouthed, "Fuck me," and seconds later I was out on the grass with you, throwing you onto your back, and tearing your boxers down around your ankles before enthusiastically jumping head first in between your legs.

FLAG STICK

spread you apart and lower my mouth down and around your now rock-hard teenage club. The scent of freshly cut grass quickly dissipates as your cock disappears down my throat, and I can taste and smell that you have been playing with it all afternoon, waiting for this. Eagerly tasting every one of your nine inches, I run my fingers through the juicy spit dripping down your balls and continue until two fingers are jammed deep inside you.

Sexy + simple
Use your fingers for plus points ++

Difficulty: easy

DOG LEG

Your hunger for my cock takes over, and you suddenly flip me over onto my back and bury your face deep in my crotch. Your lips swallow my rock hard inches, slowly at first until I feel my knob choking you as I put it deep down into your throat. I lock my legs around your head and thrust into your mouth face-fucking those hungry lips as I feel your tongue dancing around the tip of my pole, in between gasps for air.

Mouth-fucking
Great for the top to stay in control,
While lying on his back

Penetration: deep
Difficulty: medium

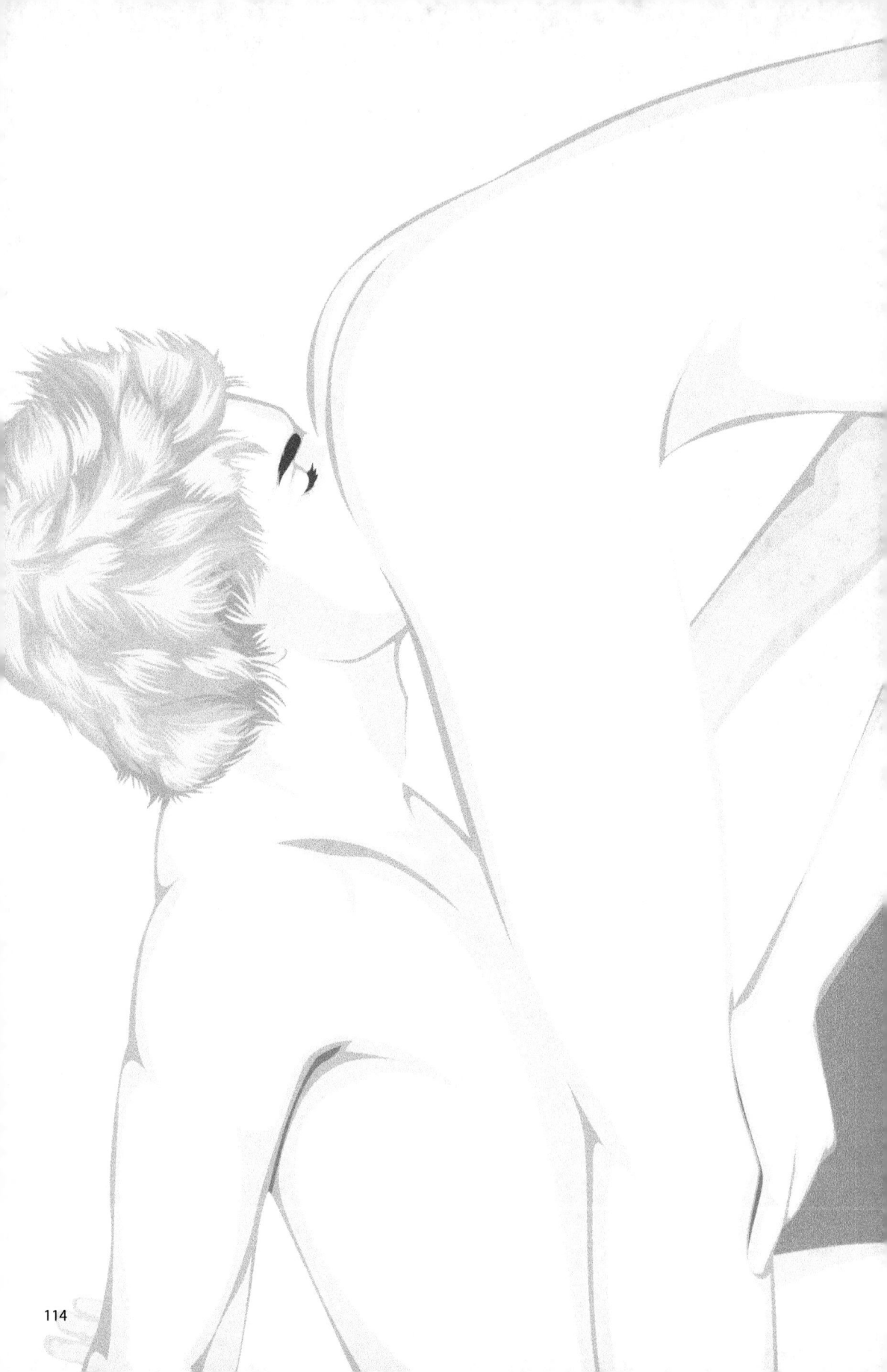

Nothing tastes sweeter than the ass of a twink bent over in your face!

Difficulty: Easy

SWEET SPOT

My appetite for your ass has become insatiable. You willingly oblige, bend over and spread your legs just wide enough for me to be able to shove my face in between your toned, smooth cheeks. Your hole tenses up as you feel me running my tongue along it, tickling you as my lips begin to suck on you. I feel the little blond hairs on the inside of your cheeks rising as I give you goose bumps. It feels like I've primed you up nicely, and you're ready for what I'm about to do to you next...

BLIND HOLE

"Sit down on top of me, pretty boy, and take my cock." You're tight and smooth, and as you inch down on me, your ass forcibly widens, barely able to fit me inside. It's such a tight squeeze, and your expression tells me just that. Your tongue finds its way into my mouth and you passionately kiss me, while thrusting your waist up and down to push me further in. You're moaning as you run your hands down my chest and play with my hard nipples, feeling my knob pulsing inches deep inside you.

What the eye can't see, the cock will feel

Penetration: medium
Difficulty: easy

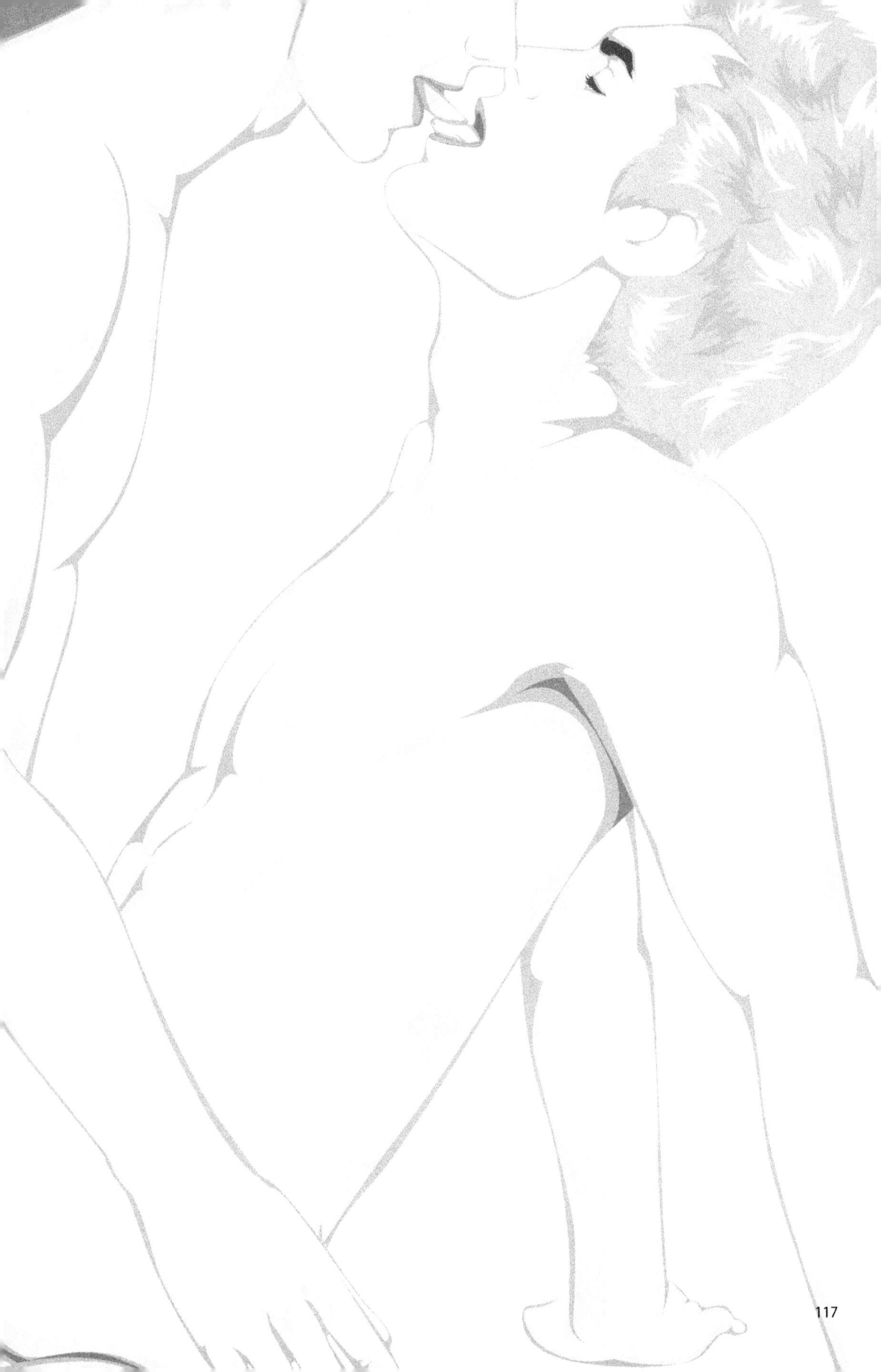

GIMMIE

I stretch my legs out and lean back, so you can take full control of my cock. Repeatedly slamming your waist onto me, you aggressively show me how much you love to take every inch. I could do this all night long, the coolness of the soft grass against my legs, your moist ass wrapped around my cock, riding me until you can't take it anymore. That's what makes you such a great fuck toy.

Stretch your legs out for deeper penetration!

Penetration: deep
Difficulty: easy

OPEN STANCE

lie back completely flat on the grass and, keeping my cock inside, you spin around, until you're sitting sideways on top, so I can force that hole apart even more. Your big teenage cock flaps around wildly like the 18th flag in the wind, covering your chest in a sticky mess, moans intensifying. You grab onto your thick teenage meat and start to jerk it hard. Watching you please yourself with your hand, I nearly blow my load instantly. Your ass suddenly tenses up around my stick and I feel your cum shooting over the grass in front, hole pulsing uncontrollably, bringing my knob that's jammed so deep inside you closer to filling you to the brim.

Lay back and enjoy the ride
Sideways penetration
is intense ++

Penetration: deep
Difficulty: medium

Balancing body weight
is sensual + intense

Penetration: medium
Difficulty: hard

BLOCK SHOT

I want to keep this intense session going, so I have no choice but to throw you off my cock and slow down. I press your back up against a tree and kneel in a wide stance underneath you, carefully placing your feet on either side of my torso. I slowly enter inside again and lean up to kiss you, as you feel my knob pushing in and pulling out of you. Sweat running down your back, your smooth hands are running down mine, caressing my shoulders. You moan in ecstasy, feeling my long pole intimately tease your moist hole. Fucking you like this couldn't be any hotter.

FOLLOW THROUGH

There's a slight chill in the air now, and the color of the sky is starting to change. We have been out here for hours and it's going to be light soon. You shiver as I gently pull out of you and lay you face down on the grass, spreading your legs apart. I lean back and press my knob up against your hole to penetrate you one last time. You eagerly push up toward me, taking me in one inch at a time, waiting for me to cum inside you. I speed up and thrust harder, moments away from a massive climax. Within seconds, I can feel myself about to burst and with one last plough, I ram my massive cock as far into you as it will go. Unable to breathe, your body tenses up as I shoot deep in your hole, gushing so hard a load so big it flows out and starts to pour down the side of your spread cheeks.

I'm completely spent and collapse beside you, where you lay in a crumpled heap, still gasping for air after I have just destroyed you.

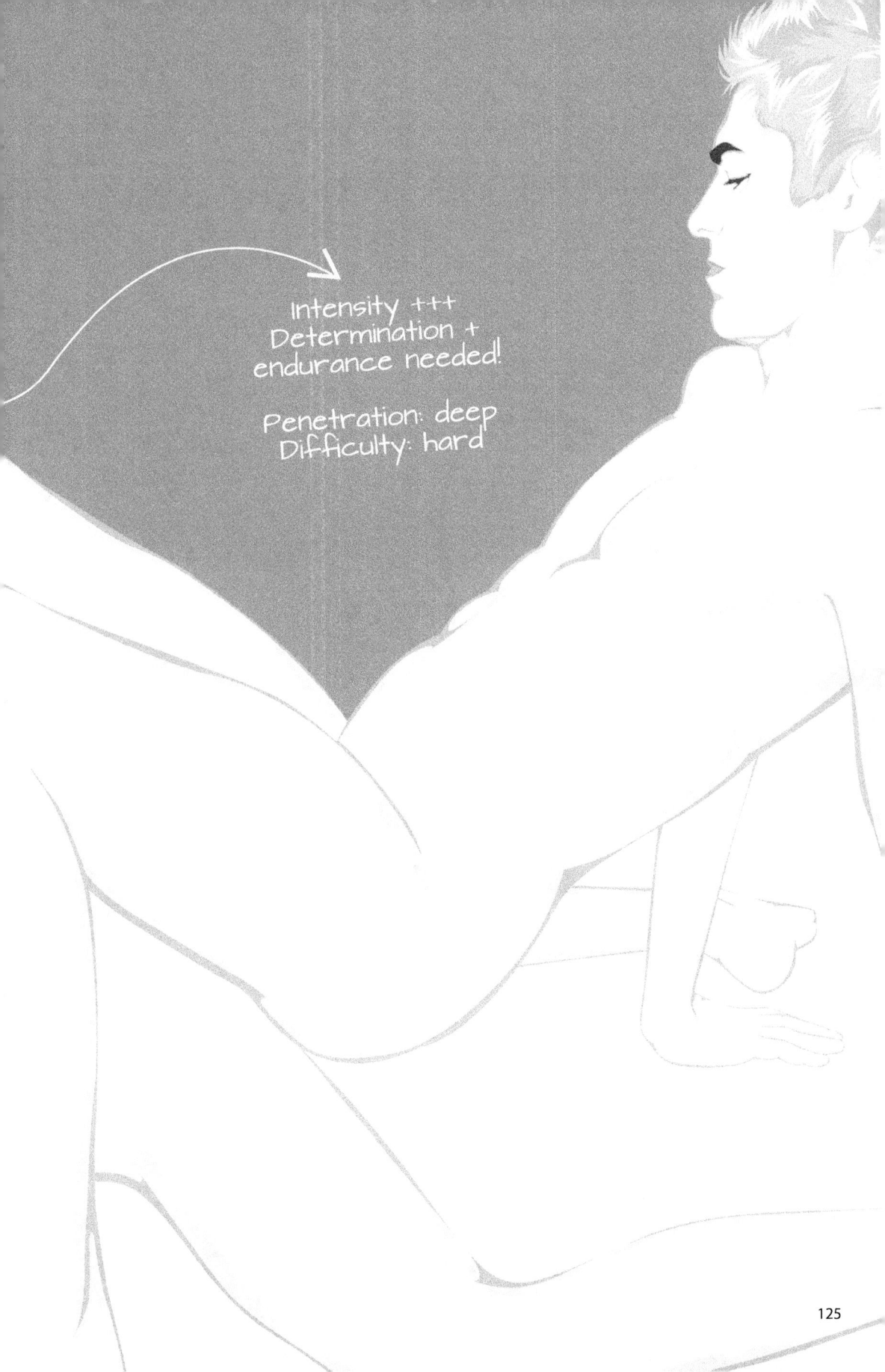

Intensity +++
Determination +
endurance needed!

Penetration: deep
Difficulty: hard

CHAPTER 8

KITE BOARDING

Extreme water sports always got my heart racing. The combination of hot sun searing my skin and crisp water splashing against me on a board always made me want to do it again. The guys out kite-boarding were all so damn hot. Each with tanned skin, board shorts and bare feet strapped to a board, aggressively being thrown around in the water, to see who could do the best tricks. The outlines of big cocks in wet shorts was always enough to make me want to just suck one dry, right then and there on the beach.

When I tangled kites with you one weekend, the one thing on my mind was that this would be the perfect opportunity to get your ass onto the beach and fuck you up for nearly wrecking my strings, by slamming a couple out in you. Despite the fact that the harness you were strapped into fit you so damn well, what was even hotter was grabbing you by the chicken loop and ripping it off. Taking the hint, you peeled off your board shorts slowly, teasing me by revealing the tight little black Speedos underneath. They barely managed to hide the outline of your meat and made your toned ass look absolutely edible.

SPREADER BAR

"**C**ome over here and sit on my face already," I teased at you while jerking my cock on the towel beside you. You looked up, glanced down at my uncut inches and planted your smooth cheeks right down on my mouth. "Go on then, suck my ass," you grinned as you reached down for my cock, rearing yourself down onto me. The combination of your salty teenage skin and your hand wrapped around my cock made me want to plough it into you.

Spread those cheeks apart and eat away! Use your ass to tease + grind

Difficulty: easy

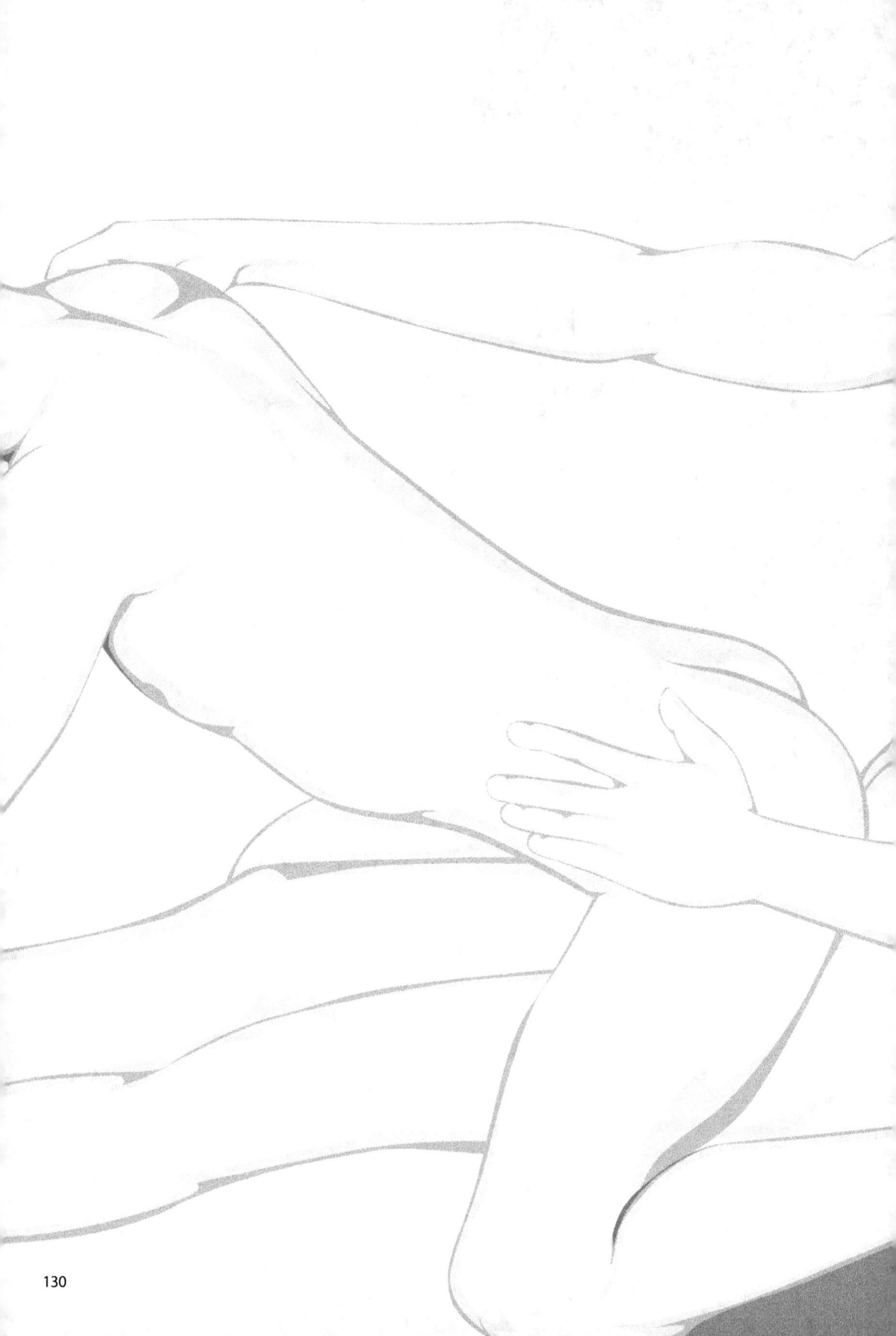

Use arms to pull back + waist for thrusting

Penetration: deep

Difficulty: medium

SCUDDING

I pushed you down onto your knees and slid you forward until your ass was pressed right up against my extremely wet knob. Leaning forward, you pushed your cheeks out at me, inviting me to take to them and rip them apart even further with both hands. I willingly obliged, allowing for my thick head to force its way in slowly and painfully. I could feel you wince and tense up—it was going to be a tight squeeze. Inch by inch, I felt you wrapping your tight ass around my eager cock, my foreskin ripping back as I slid in deeper.

HOOKED IN

It was slow to start, but the reward of penetrating your teenage ass was enough to make me want to aggressively dominate your smooth, tanned body. I pulled you up onto your knees and, kneeling behind you, entered you again, pushing in a bit faster this time. Grabbing you with both arms I hooked right into you, just the way I like. The slamming got rougher and so intense that your knees began to lift off the ground as your cock burst and shot cum all over the sand in front of us.

'Beginners' position to enjoy the moment in

Penetration: medium
Difficulty: easy

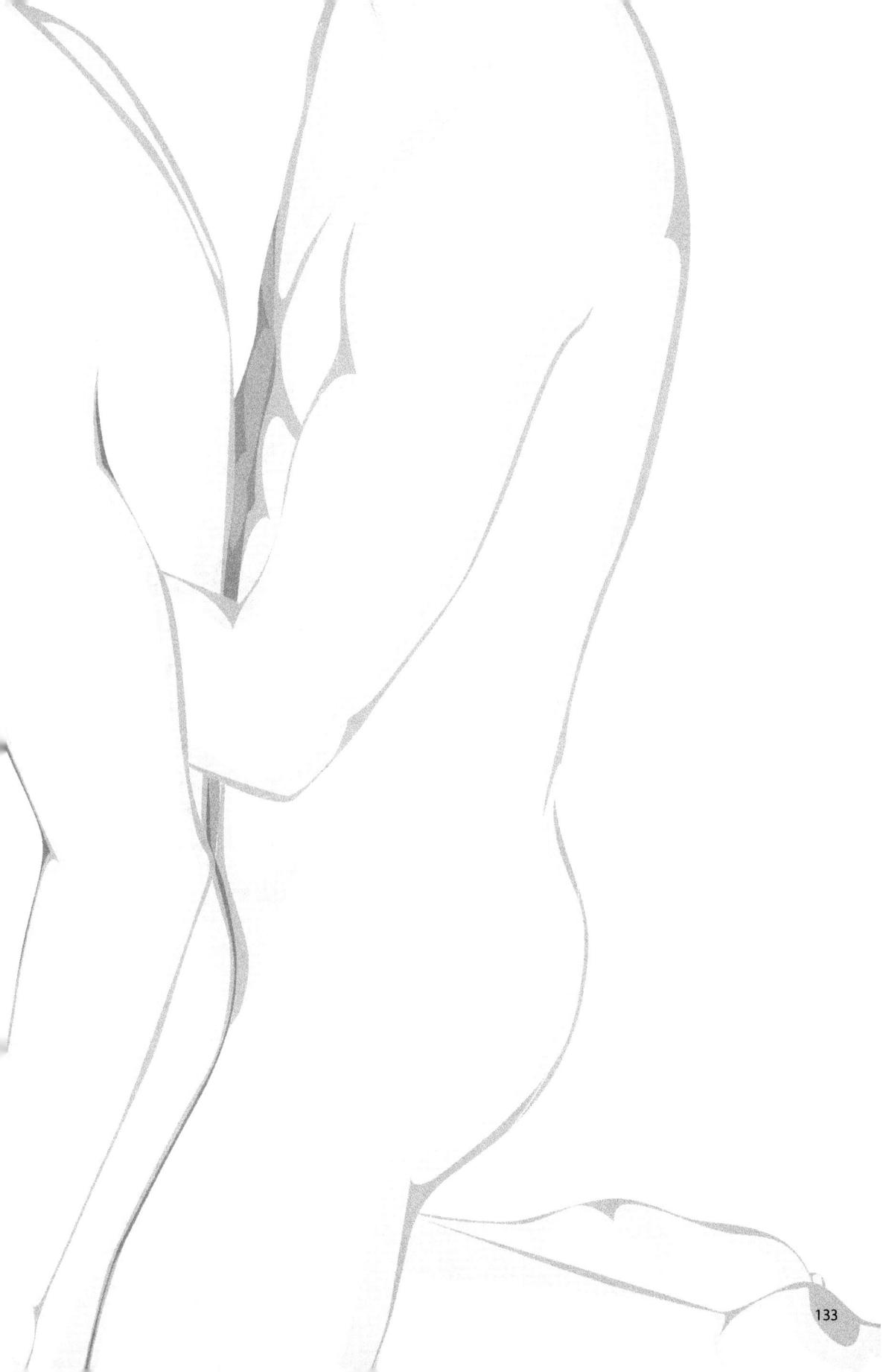

TEA-BAGGING

Feeling your tight hole contracting around my cock as you blow everywhere makes me want to bust my nut already. But I want you to swallow this first load and taste my thick cum. I pull out and shove my cock in your face, as you lie there with a wanting look and watch me slap you around with it, the taste of your ass covering your lips. It slides all the way down the back of your throat in one swift move, making you gag and choke on it. A couple of plunges later and you're swallowing my large load. I hold it jammed down there until I'm sure you have swallowed every last drop.

For one decent mouthful. Intense but controlled face fucking

Penetration: deep
Difficulty: medium

135

BODY DRAGGING

'm not done with you yet. My cock is still throbbing hard and eager to get back into that sand covered ass of yours. My tingling knob still wet, I jam into you sideways. My urges take over and with one big thrust I slam all the way into you. I'm on top and completely in control and I pound away at you like the waves crashing on the shore. Fucking you so hard I want to destroy your ass so you keep feeling me for days to come.

Sideways = intense

Penetration: deep
Difficulty: medium

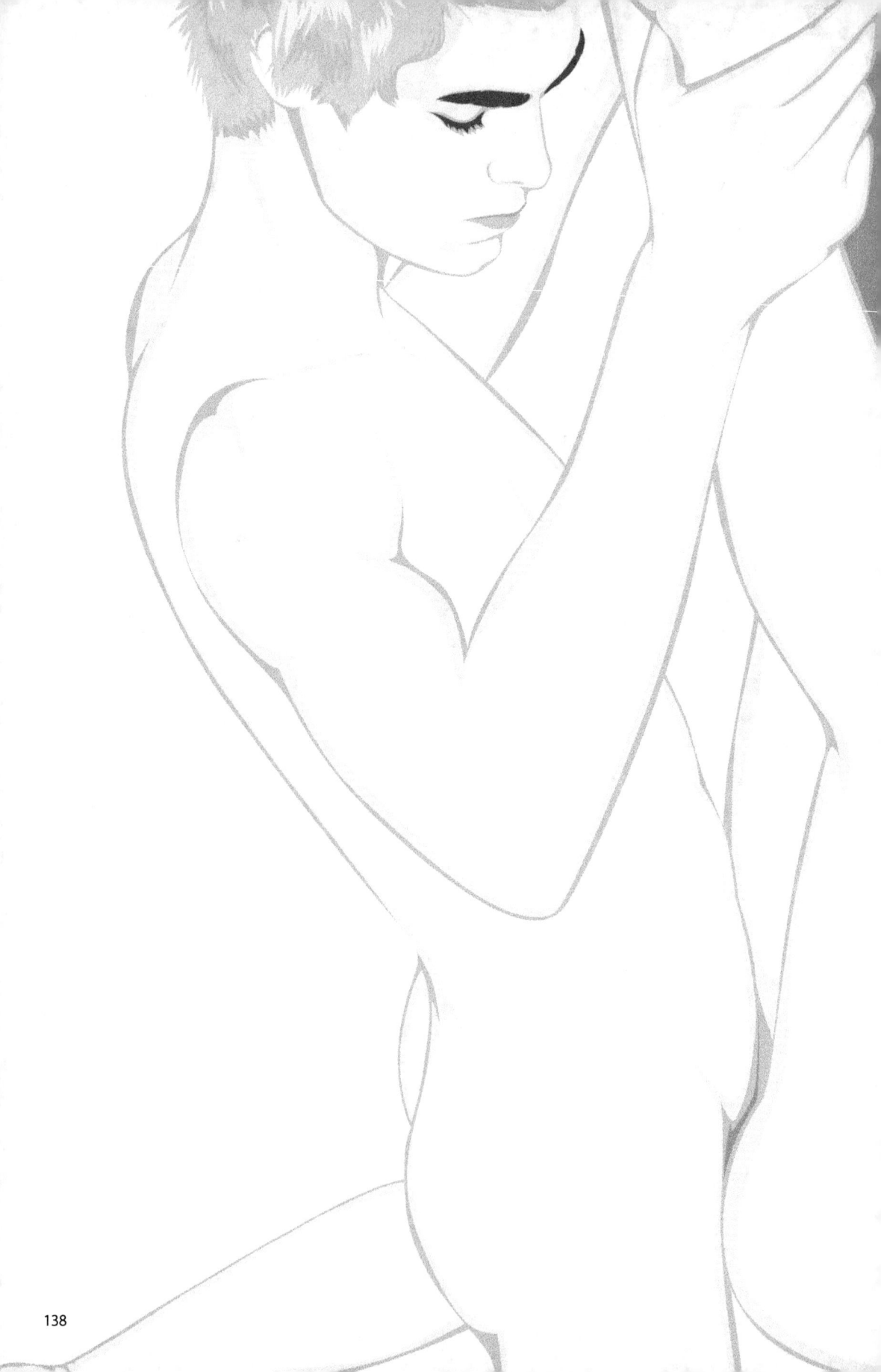

POWER ZONE

That's exactly why I flip you on your back and do just that. I've worked up an appetite and you're going to know exactly what it means to feel the force of my cock plunge further and deeper into you. I spread your legs wide and hold them apart, while ravaging your little ass. You're a hot little stud, and boys like you deserve to be punished hard. It's hard to punish you though when you love taking it so much. Just means I need to keep ploughing into you, forcing you to feel every inch harder and faster until you're gasping for air and screaming my name, until you can barely take it anymore and you're begging me to stop.

Wider spread = deeper in

Penetration: deep
Difficulty: medium

LAY LINE

pull out of you as I'm about to blow, stopping just in time. In one last effort, I pick you up and throw you straight onto your back again, over the buggy and tell you to hold on tight, as I pick your legs right back up, straight into the air in front of me, and slide myself all the way into you. I absolutely slam you, so hard you can hear my low hanging balls slapping against you. Suddenly cum starts shooting out of your cock, hitting you in the face and drenching you. I immediately pull out and let my own load continue to cover you from head to toe, leaving you a sticky mess. I can't help but to slap you around with my bulging cock a couple of times just to remind you of what you just had inside that boy hole.

Go hard or go home!
Drive hard, deep + go for gold

Penetration: deep
Difficulty: medium

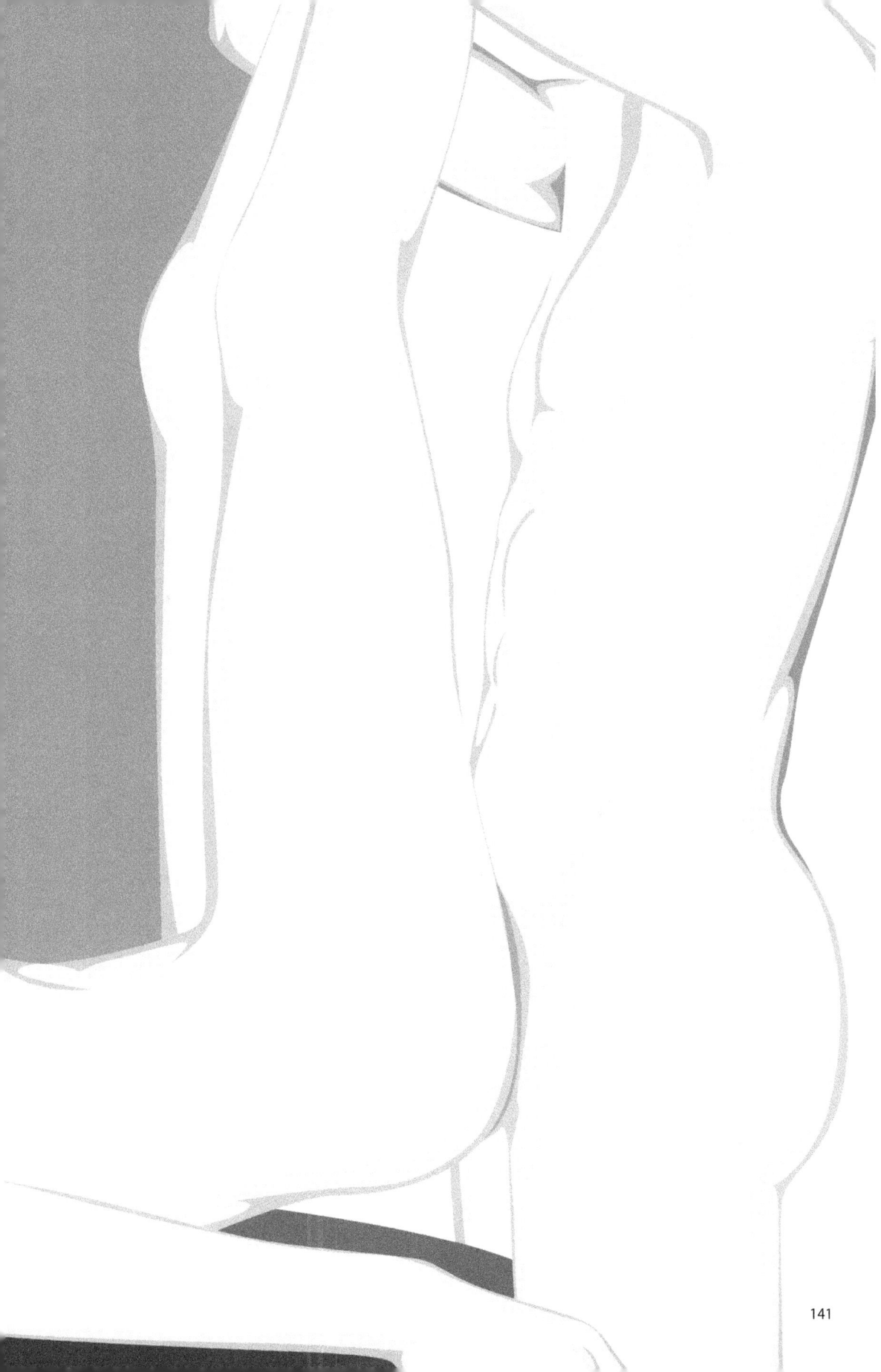

DON'T FORGET THESE 101 FUCKING RULES OF FUCKING

You've just spent all this time playing and prepping to get to fifth base, so no pressure – but know what you're doing!
Yes, practice makes perfect, and like any skill it does take time to get it right.
Chances are either you or your playmate has done it before – so as a team you should be right to hit a home run. If it is a first round for both, then get to know the rules of this game and how to play first. Amateur porn videos were made for you!

The Three Second Rule: Don't be the Three Second Guy! Don't let it be over before it even begins –
If you're packing a three day stash of frustration, or turned on enough to just need to let it out, DO THAT FIRST, break and then start - not three seconds after you begin. There's enough foreplay to get rid of that awkwardly massive first load, first. And you might just find a neat place to put it.

Sexual Anxiety?
Relax. Your playmate should be someone you are comfortable with. Remember above all that sex should be fun.

Make sure you're up to the challenge.
You should be rock hard and ready before you even try anything.

Fresh out of sex drive or just can't get it up? Perk up and pack some extra punch by adding some natural stimulants to your diet.
Fruits such as watermelon and pomegranate are jammed full of nature's viagra and can really take your potency to the next level. Have you had a Banana Smoothie recently?

Don't just shove it in! Unless he wants you to...
Foreplay was designed to make sex that much easier and more enjoyable by the time you make it to fifth base.
Never forget the golden rule – Always pitch a slow ball first and go easy, until you know how hard he is able to catch. Tear a muscle in there and it's game over.

If you're on top:
Pick a position you understand and can comfortably work with to start, and take control. You're the ACTIVE TOP for a reason, so FUCK LIKE YOU MEAN IT.

If your playmate's on top: Let him take charge and be there to help him find the right angle and balance
Adjust your legs or butt enough to make for smooth sailing. And smooth sailing ALWAYS means rough riding. He is on top for a reason after all, so why not just lie back and enjoy him. Let him show you just how much he can be in control.

Pick a position, any position. Just not the one you don't know how to do.
Using different positions to break it up is the way to go. Having 5-10 up your sleeve that you are both good at and can shift between in the heat of the moment will impress your playmate more than you think. Truth be told, there's ninety-something for you to start getting fresh with right here.

Practice makes perfect: Learning new positions will make sure that you keep your edge while keeping it fresh for your playmate
Don't fuck it up though – get to know and understand the position first and by yourself before you even attempt to bring it to the bedroom. Under-promise and over-deliver...Tell your playmate you want to try something out on him for the first time and remembering it's a team effort, help each other out so you can get it right. Injuries aren't fun and a team captain never lets his teammate down, does he?

Say it with your mouth and not your ass: If it hurts, DO NOT arch your back or inch your butt away. This is one of the great and frustrating failures of fuck.
As he takes his position and starts to push upward and inward, it's not the time to play catch me if you can all over the bed, unless of course that is in fact what you're playing. Foreplay is designed to do the breaking in. So if it's still hurting head back to base one (or two, three or four) and give the foreplay the attention it deserves. On the other hand, if his massive ego is in fact as big as you're finally realizing, then you might just have to grin and bear it. Or call a time-out instead.

LUBE LUBE LUBE 4 Smooth Sailing: This really speaks for itself.
Enough foreplay, done the right way should mean both playmates are spit covered and dripping with excitement enough to get going. If you're jumping into a wetsuit, you'll be sure to find that a high quality lube will soon become your second best friend.

CHAPTER 9

NFL

Being Australian, I never really understood American football, but like any teenager exploring the Internet, hot images of college football jocks always turned me on. It was our first Halloween in America and when you showed up to pick me up for the trick-or-treat party we were going to that night, I nearly blew in my pants when I found you standing at the front door, dressed as the football jock that I'd been fantasizing about for years! The tight-fitting pants and shoulder gear you were wearing were enough to get my mind racing. It was just like looking at one of the Abercrombie poster boys just begging to be torn into. The outline of your thick teenage treat was hard to hide in your tight pants and I could hardly wait to slide them down your long legs after I got you alone.

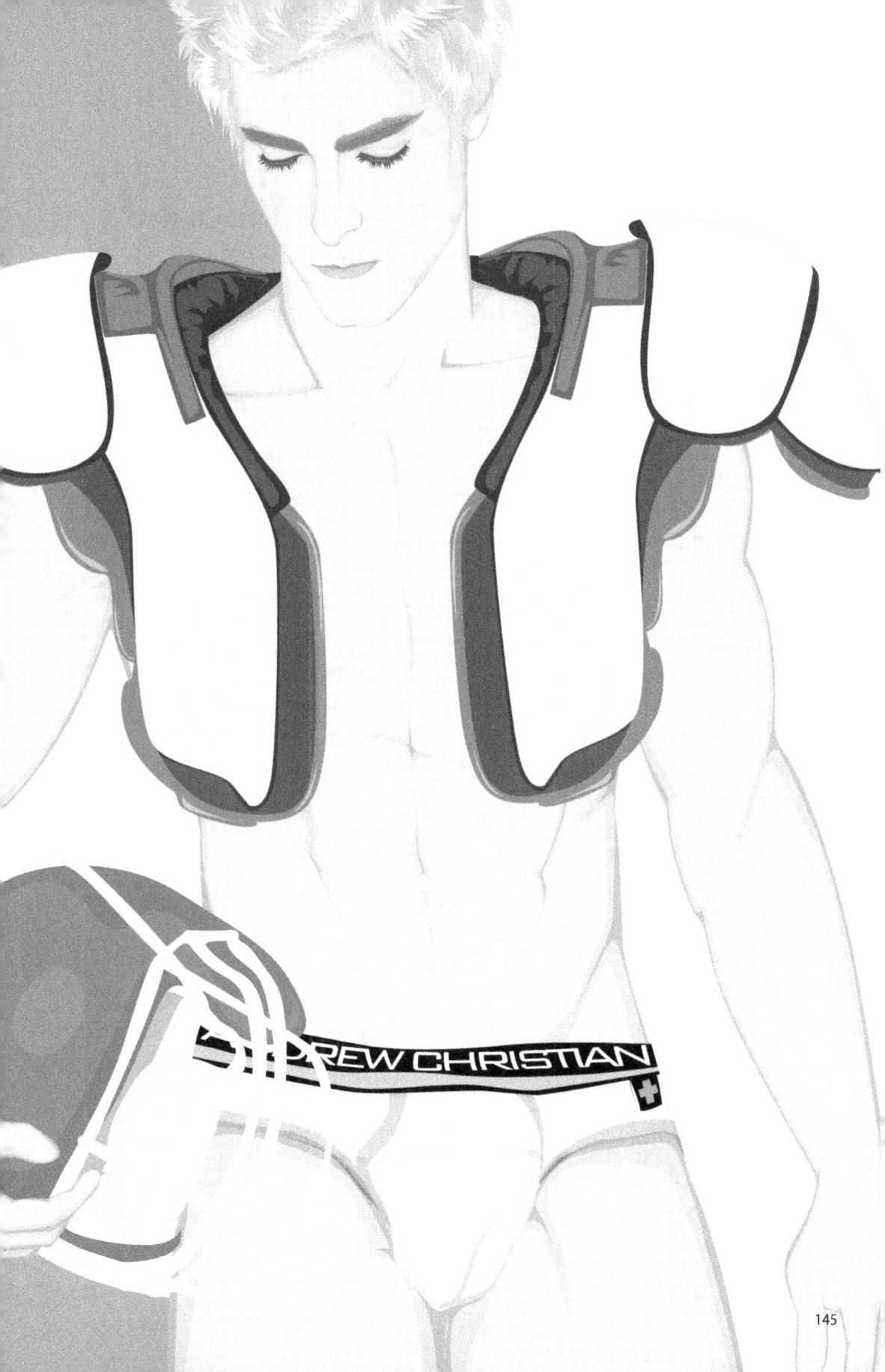

DOUBLE COVERAGE

We left the party early, and you insisted on taking me straight back to your place. The moment you shut the door, I pinned you to the wall and took my time running my hands up and down your bare chest and grabbing onto your shoulder pads. Sliding down on my knees in front of you, I aggressively rubbed my face up and down against the hard outline through your tight nylon pants, getting more turned on by the second, worshipping the hot football jock standing in front of me. I couldn't help but pull your pants down to your ankles and let those nine hard inches out. "Catch me if you can," you taunted, before tearing up the stairs, ass just visible hanging out of your Florida State jersey and your cock bouncing with every step. Seconds later I ran up the stairs behind you and followed you into your room, where I found you waiting on the edge of the bed, keen to get on top of me and bury your face between my legs. As I felt you wrap your lips around my cock, I couldn't help but grab your cheeks and tear into your ass with my tongue. I locked my legs around your head and made you gag on my thick inches, which only made me want to make you taste them even more.

Stimulation both ways -
The best kind!

Perfect pre-play foreplay
for ass + cock
Difficulty: easy

MOUTH PIECE

want to grab you by the hair and force you to eat my cock. Sitting at the edge of your bed I do just that and tell you to get down on your knees in front of me and suck it. I lean back and enjoy feeling your mouth slide up and down my pole, while I rub up against yours with my left foot. I can feel you lubing me up nicely, and as I slide my toe up against your already wet hole, I know exactly what I want to do next.

CORNERBACK

On the floor and between your legs was right where my eager cock was heading. You willingly oblige, spreading your legs wide enough for me to be able to get in between them. Seems I wasn't the only one ready to go for it. Both lying on our sides, it's the perfect position to be able to watch you squirm as I tease your ass with my hard knob, threatening to force it apart. You had a good idea of how big I was from all the previous times I had destroyed your ass, and as I begin to slide into you, I feel your hand nervously wrap around my pole, excitedly feeling each inch push its way inside you.

Sexy + sensual
with an awesome view
Penetration: medium
Difficulty: medium

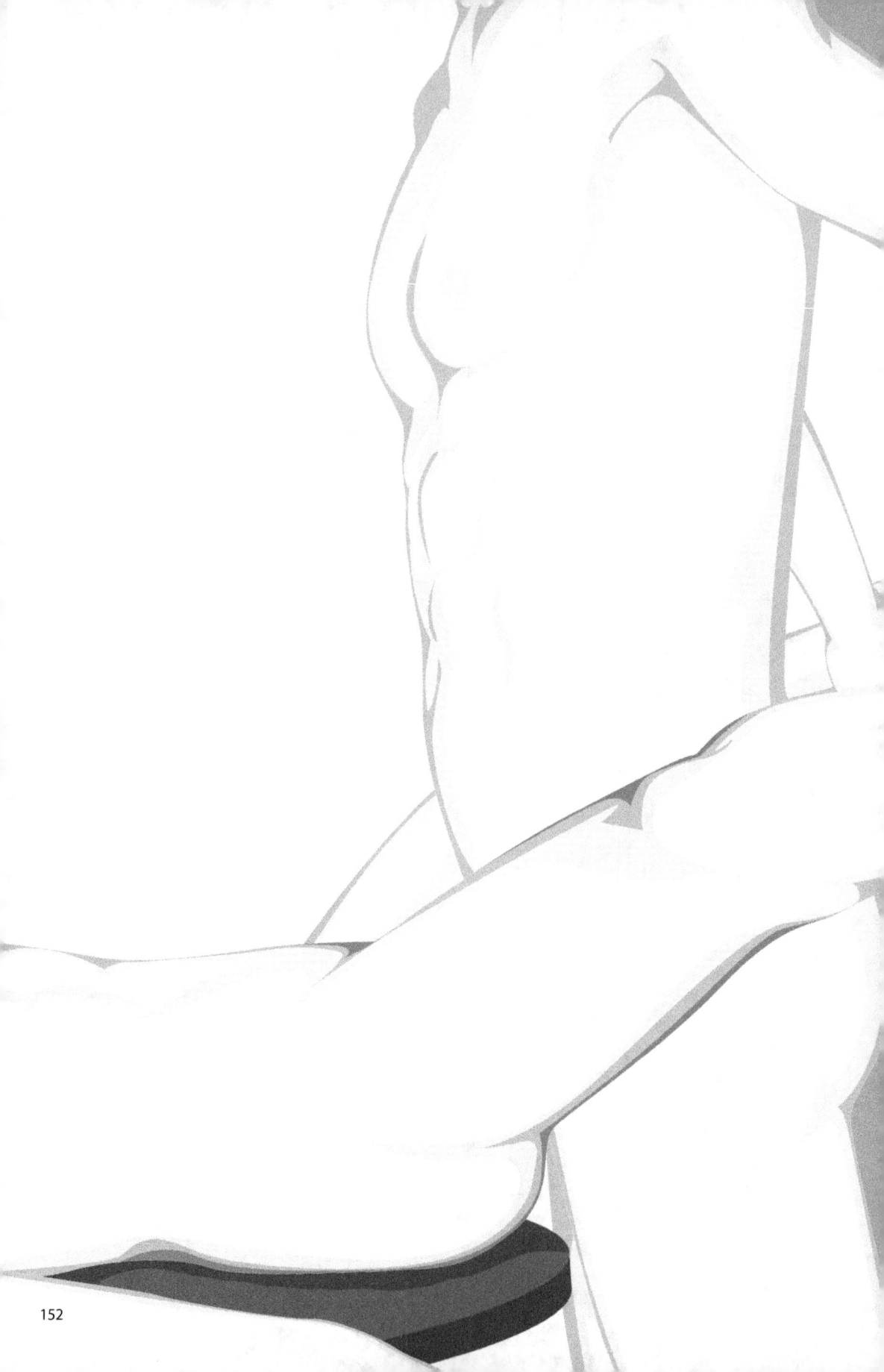

Thrust hard, spread wide and go deep - It's the perfect working height

Penetration: deep
Difficulty: medium

GOING FOR IT

After breaking you in, I pick you up and throw you on the desk. Lying on your back staring up at me, waiting for me to make my next move, I grab your legs and push them apart so I can get right back inside you. Slamming you from waist height I feel myself forcing into your ass, going deeper with each plunge. It's still a tight squeeze to get in as far as I want, and I feel you obediently swallowing another inch and another with each one of my aggressive thrusts. By the time I'm all the way in and slamming into you, you've finally eased up and start begging me to go deeper. I push every one of my inches as deep inside as they can possibly go, spreading your legs wide apart, destroying your hole.

END AROUND

I pick you up, throw you on the bed and lie on my back with my legs up in the air. Making you sit on top of my cock, I can feel it forcing its way into you, while you push down on me so hard it hurts. As my rock hard pole gets jammed deeper inside you, I feel you squirm from the pressure of every last inch you're being forced to take. You excitedly ride up and down on me, moaning loudly and balancing awkwardly, never slowing down, even as I'm about to burst. The pressure on my knob is immense and when you feel my cock start to swell, you plunge down on it even harder, making me blow so hard and deep inside you, it makes you instantly shoot all over your bedroom floor. There's so much cum, I can feel it running down your cock and dribbling onto my balls.

Advanced reverse penetration
Balance + skill + fitness is a must

Penetration: deep
Difficulty: hard

UP THE MIDDLE

'm pumped! What was probably one of the best orgasms of my life has given my cock a mind of its own. Still that hard, it seems like it's never going down. Now that you've had a taste, the gleam in your eye tells me straight away that your ass is all mine—even for the rest of the night, which is why I love sleepovers so much. That would explain why you're down on all fours in front of me. I kneel down behind you and taste the cum dripping out of your abused hole, and my still hard cock continues to drip all over your floor.

HUDDLE

It seems as though you're ready for a bedtime story, but the cuddles I have in mind are going to do everything but put you to sleep. Back in bed and under the covers, I press up against you and gently slide into your warm and moist hole. You begin to breathe a little heavier as I slide about halfway in and just stay there inside you, feeling my inches throbbing as they press against your inner walls. It feels good enough to want to stay in there for the rest of the night, and as I press closer up against you, I don't think you mind at all falling asleep with my cock pounding away gently inside your teenage hole.

After-sex cuddles are the best, especially when the sex doesn't stop!

Penetration: medium
Difficulty: easy

CHAPTER 10

RUGBY

You were standing at the other end of the tram when I got on one night, and I used the empty space down at your end as an excuse to stand next to you. My eyes were instantly drawn to your tall physique, dressed in some sports gear, obviously coming home from practice. I soon realized that your eyes were staring down at my bulge, which had started to grow—and quite rapidly—as soon as I caught a whiff of the sweat-stained jersey you had on. You seemed fascinated by how big my bulge was getting, and it only took a second to realize what you were smirking at.

Slightly embarrassed I went to cover it, but then you moved in my direction and after accidentally grinding up against it took the seat right next to where I was standing. Your sillage was driving me wild. Enthusiastically I realize that where you're sitting, my package was almost right up against your face. Cheeks a bit flushed and chest pounding faster than before, I took the hint and let my inches quickly fill up the rest of the front of my pants. Catching a glimpse of my eager anticipation, you cheekily pulled my cock out of my pants and wrapped your lips around them.

HIGH SHOT

It wasn't long until the tram had come to the last stop and we were the last two left on it. I had little choice but to follow you off it, which you seemed to have no issue with, smirking as you looked over your shoulder to make sure I was following you.

We walked a couple of minutes before reaching a park. You wasted no time grabbing onto my crotch with one hand while skillfully ripping my pants open with the other to reveal my hard cock, which was already moist as hell. I could see this impressed you, and seconds later your pants were wrapped around your ankles and your throbbing knob was staring me in the face. I wasted no time and pushed you back against the picnic table, throwing your legs over my shoulders and rubbing some spit into your craving hole, and began to inch into you

Solid starting position -
comfortable and in control

Penetration: medium
Difficulty: easy

Teamwork makes for sexy body angles!

Penetration: deep (deliberate)

Difficulty: hard

OVERLAP

You were an enthusiastic player, and the horny look in your eye told me you wanted to play ball—and hard. I pulled out of you, jumped up onto the table I had just leaned you against, and told you to climb on top of me, throwing your legs back over my shoulders. You obliged, excitedly sliding down on top of me, fast and deep, and started to thrust deliberately onto my cock, throwing your head back and moaning louder the harder you went. This was not what I had in mind when I jumped on the tram an hour earlier, that's for sure.

OVER THE TOP

I don't think I could ever get enough of your young, tight, teenage ass bouncing on top of me—and it seemed like you were just getting started. This belongs on the park bench, so you can continue to ride up and down on top of me like the energizer bunny you are, while I get even deeper inside you. With your legs spread on either side of me again, I can see in between them and watch my thick cock slamming in and out of your ass as you willingly take every inch over and over again. It's equally hot watching yours bounce around too, drooling all over the two of us.

Trust + skill + coordination will make this a winning position

Penetration deep Difficulty hard

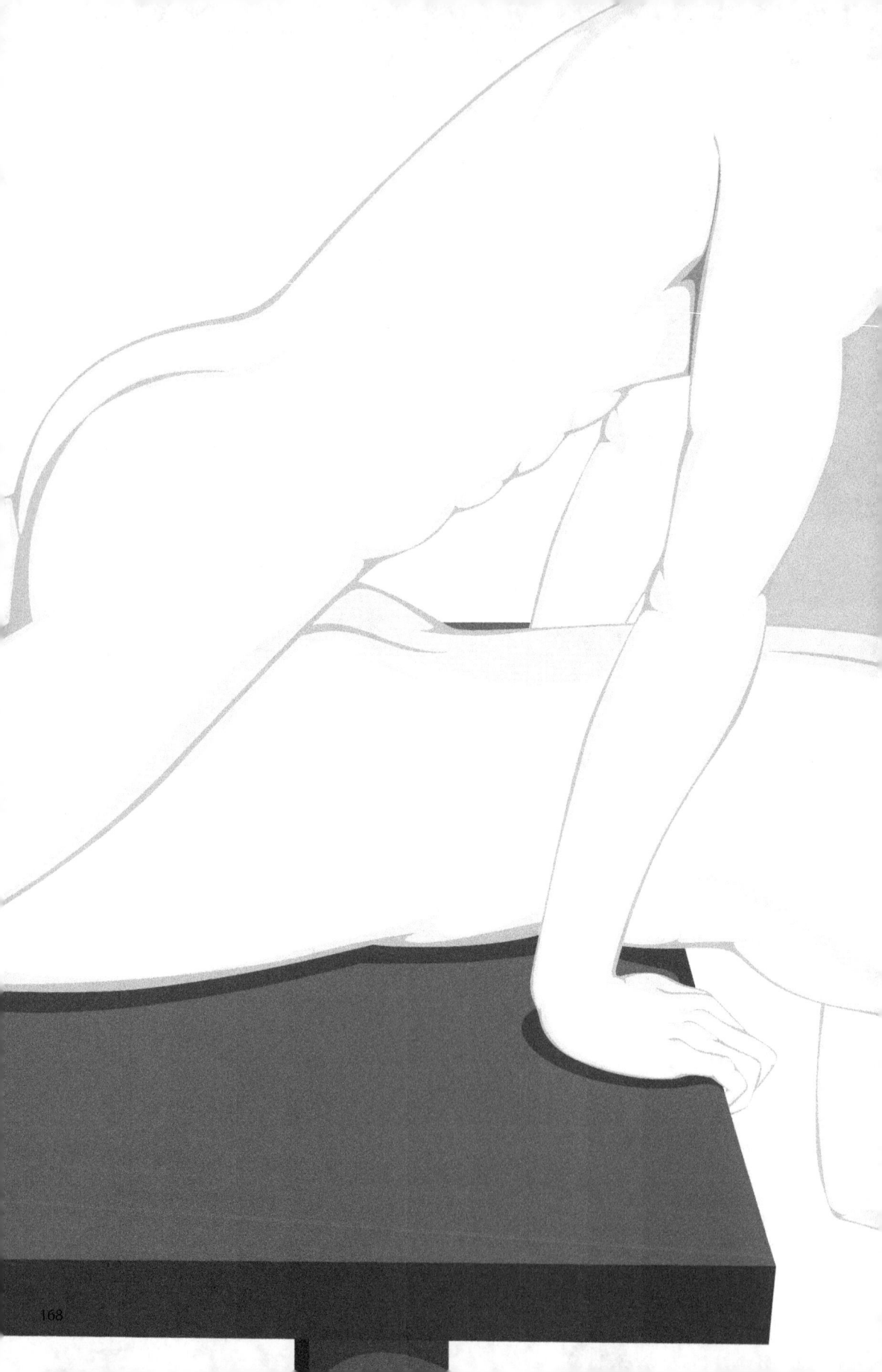

SPEAR TACKLE

Your big teenage meat has actually turned me on enough to want to take a turn getting it slammed into me. You slide off me and I lean face-down off the side of the park bench, letting you enter me from behind. You're so keen to put that impressive cock of yours to good use, and soon you're pounding me fast and rough, occasionally pulling all the way out just to make sure I can feel your thick head penetrate me again as you slam it all the way back in. I feel your knob expand inside me as you begin to blow, gushing hard and filling me up with what felt like days' worth of your massive teenage load. You let out a few deep moans and roll off, onto the grass and spread your legs, reminding me that I have some unfinished business.

Easy + intense + hot
Perfect 'beginners'
position

Penetration: medium
Difficulty: easy

Intense +++
feels as hot as it looks
Hands are free to explore.
Penetration: deep
Difficulty: medium

FULLBACK

I push myself in behind you, wrapping your spread legs around my waist. Pulling you closer onto me, I push inside you and get straight to work repaying the favor. I can feel your cum inside me and want you to feel mine inside you. I can take my time in this position, thrusting into you slow, then fast, while you lie back and enjoy each deliberate entry into you. I run one hand down your sweat-covered chest and play with your hard nipple, while I use my other hand to finger you, my cock pushing deeper inside.

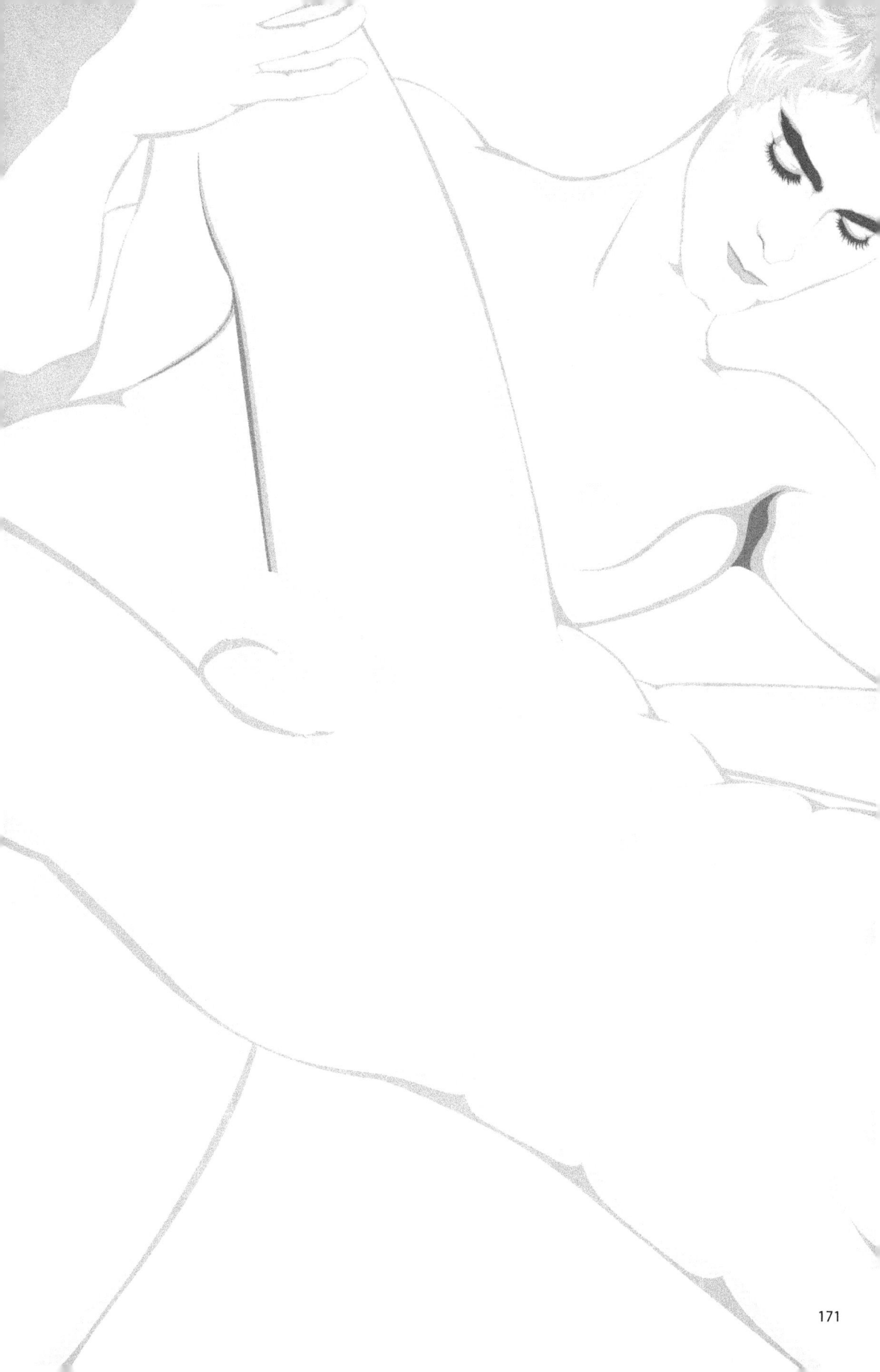

UNDER THE STICKS

inally the combination of your sporadic moans together with finger and cock slamming into you at the same time makes me want to give you exactly what you have been waiting for. Rolling you onto your back, I hold both feet up in the air and pull your ass up high enough to stick my knob straight in. I tease you with it a couple of times, while you're lying there eagerly anticipating what's about to come next. The scent of your feet and the wetness of your hole stimulating my sensitive uncut head was about all I could take before exploding into you, just far enough to fill you with each of the seven shots it took to empty my load. I knew that I had filled your appetite, and I was totally satisfied knowing that you would feel me inside you for the rest of the night.

Finishing position creates maximum enjoyment for both

Penetration: medium
Difficulty: medium

Hello.
This is a note
to remind you:

When fucking in public
never get
Busted.

Use a familiar place
that you know how to get out of, easily

Less is more
(board shorts + thongs)
clothes that are easy to get off and put back on in a hurry

Don't leave anything behind
On a dark beach at night, your phone will lose itself

Always keep an eye out
it's a public place

If you get busted, be polite about it
Chances are police will let you off with a warning

CHAPTER 11

SNOWBOARDING

've always wanted to fuck in the snow. The very thought of sex in an environment so different to the East Coast beaches where I'd spent my teenage years playing with all my friends still arouses me. I imagine a bare, tanned ass against the white snow, needing to be pounded hard just to stay warm. So when the opportunity came to invite a friend up to try out some snowboarding for the weekend, you came to mind straight away. I envisioned putting sex together with a snowboard and had every intention of taking extreme sports to a whole new level. The anticipation of the few days out in the snow was already sending dirty chills down the inside of the thick snow pants I was trying on for size.

***

You got out of the shower, butt naked and waving your tight little ass around, making sure to draw attention to the fact that you were going commando, sliding into your snow gear with nothing underneath. That just meant that your big meat would be rubbing against the inside of your snow pants all day, and you would probably be hard the whole time. Just before you slid your pants all the way up, you told me to spit on my fingers so you could rub them up against your ass. "I want you to get me wet," you told me, "so you can tear me apart in the snow later." Between your tease and the sunny weather, it sounded like we were going to have an unforgettable day snowboarding.

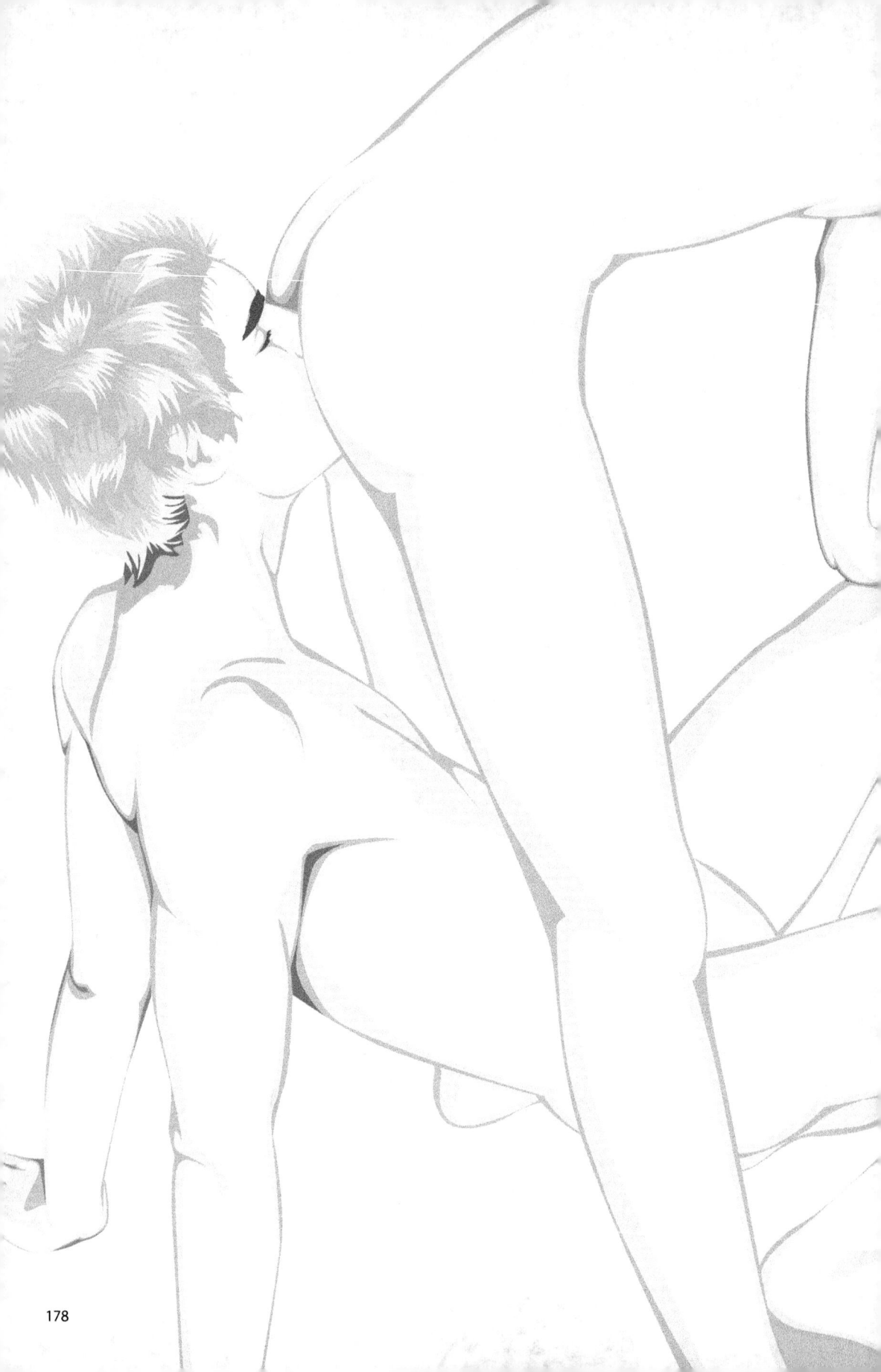

CANADIAN BACON AIR

We spent a lot of time falling around in the snow, and each time you fell flat on your ass I was instantly drawn to recall the two wet fingers I slid in there this morning, and how you weren't wearing anything under your snow pants. Pretty sure it was time to give you exactly what you were asking for. I ripped your pants a little way down and leaned back on my hands and feet telling you to rear your ass up in my face. Jamming my tongue in between your cheeks I was half expecting to see that hot little butt of yours steaming in the cold air.

Use the flexible position you're bent in to grind up into your playmate's face

Difficulty: easy

HO HO

You had managed to wedge your board pretty deep into the snow on your last effort stacking off it. I eagerly threw you onto your back, snow pants halfway down around your knees. I sat at the edge of your board, making sure to keep your smooth little ass off the snow. Grabbing your feet and flinging them over my shoulders I edged closer to you, pressing my hard knob up to your eagerly anticipating hole. I began to slide into you and could feel by your short, heavy breaths that you're just as tight as I felt you earlier this morning. Lucky for you I can only go slow from this angle, which means you can enjoy lying there and feeling me forcing you apart slowly and deliberately.

Deliberate + visually
stimulating
A position to appeal to all
the senses

Penetration: medium
Difficulty: medium

CRAIL GRAB

Sitting on your board, pounding you out in the snow is getting me pretty worked up, and I'm in the mood to get a bit more violent with your ass. I grab higher on your legs and lift you slightly up onto me, into a position where I can take more control and pick up the pace. From here I can spread your legs wider apart and shove more aggressively into you. I've had to rip your snow pants off now, so I've got to be sure to pummel you solidly and do the deed—so I can slide those pants back on when I'm done. I'm deep inside your warm, moist ass and have no problem blowing in you within seconds. You let out a few moans as you feel my hot cum fill you. Throwing your pants on even more eagerly, you dig your board out of the snow and jump on it again, smirking at me to follow you.

Get in there and use that boy
He should be asking for it by now!

Penetration: medium
Difficulty: medium

SUITCASE AIR

You're a hot shithead with your board and in your snow gear, but completely suck at it all the same. It's funny watching you fall off every five minutes. The next time you face-plant in the snow, I decide to keep you there for a little while and have another go at you from behind. You're on all fours when I push your face down into the snow and rip your pants off, peeling them down far enough to expose your tanned ass, just as I had imagined this would be. I crouch down and squat into you, holding my hard pole straight in front, so I can slide it right into you. I feel your ass seize up around my big cock and take every inch as I sink it into you. It pleases me to feel it deep inside you, but it's never enough, and I want to go deeper.

Push his face down and put in a solid effort!

Penetration: deep
Difficulty: hard

ROAST BEEF

pull out and use both hands to swiftly drop your pants to your ankles again, pushing you back into the snow. Your legs start to shiver from the cold, but I don't care. I spread your lanky legs apart and sit on top of you, before shoving a handful of snow in between your cheeks and forcing it into your hole. So keen to explore the sensation of the freezing ice against my hot skin sliding inside you, I begin to force my thick meat into your snow-lubed hole, which has completely puckered from the cold. Your freezing ass must be numb from the ice by now as my pressure jamming into you becomes more and more violent, and you just lie there and take it, occasionally whimpering without putting up much of a fight. The grinding is so intense against my rock hard inches, that in a matter of minutes my knob swells again and suddenly dumps a massive second load into you. I should probably let you put your bottoms back on now, before your cold little dick freezes up on me.

Keep a good balance +
a consistent thrust
(strong thighs needed!)
Penetration: deep
Difficulty: hard

STIFFY

You're totally pleased, but I can tell you're freezing by now too. I've got one more load for you today, so we head back to the cabin and I let you defrost by the fireplace. You look like you have something else in mind, though. The second we get back inside you've stripped off your gear, the cheekiest look in your eye. I've seen that look before. You jump up on the little coffee table and tell me to get up behind you. I run my tongue between your cheeks and up your back as I get in position behind you, catching a taste of the two loads I've already put inside. I'm instantly stiff again, and in a swift move grab onto your waist and own that ass. I slam in and out violently, in a trance as I feel your fully loaded hole eat every one of my inches again and again. I pull out and push in over and over just so I can watch my thick knob penetrating your used hole again with each tingling thrust.

Stand up to the challenge and spread wide

Wide = really deep

Difficulty: hard

TUCK KNEE

Finally I can't take it anymore, and I have to cum in you again. Picking you up, I carry you over to the bed and throw you on your back. As I tuck my knee behind you and thrust one last time into you, I feel my cock explode. You're furiously jerking your long hard cock at the same time, and tell me to wrap my hand around it as you blow. You shower us both in your thick juice and don't let me pull out of you until I've gone completely soft. By the time I pull out, you've passed out and I lie there for a while running my fingers around your abused hole, watching my three achievements slowly dripping out.

For a deep-seeded climax this is the way to go!

Intense +++
Bodies naturally fit together

Penetration deep
Difficulty easy

CHAPTER 12

SURFING

I felt something shift in my board shorts when you showed up at my place this morning to pick me up for a surf down at the beach. You were standing in bare feet at my front door when you knocked, wearing nothing but a cap, on backwards, and a pair of loose fitting boardies, revealing your solid tan line and a glimpse of your pale, white ass cheek. I didn't need any convincing to throw my board in the back seat and jump in the front of your ride next to you. "Hope you're ready for an awesome day at the beach," you shouted at me over the loud music, speeding toward the beach, hand on your crotch and cheeky gleam in your eye.

***

I walk behind you, instinctively, every time we're on the beach together. I get totally turned on watching your tanned teenage legs walking on the sand, your ass poking out of the top of your shorts and a board tucked under your arm.

It's not long till we're both out splashing around on our boards. My cock gets pretty big early on, watching you face down on your board, boy feet splashing in and out of the water, soaked and oversized board shorts unable to stay on high enough to cover the cheeky white ass from the rest of your tanned, athletic body.

193

Classic 'beginner's' position
Boy on top can work at his
own pace

Penetration: medium
Difficulty: easy

KNEEBOARDING

B
eing the shithead that you are, you waste no time knocking me off my board and inviting me onto yours. My hand instantly finds its way up your shorts, where my wet fingers start to play with your tight hole. You flash me a smirk and return the favor by wrapping your hand around my already throbbing pole. You waste no time stroking me hard, and I'm not going to either. I grab your shorts, jump back on my board and make you paddle back to the shore naked. I paddle close behind so I can watch you on your board with your legs spread. I can see in between your cheeks, I'm seriously hard and ready to get in there.

Back in the shallows there's enough room on your long board for the two of us. Before I know it, you've flipped me on my back and you're pushing your cheeks apart. I don't even need to spit on my cock because it's already dripping with pre-cum. I watch you throw your head back and slowly slide down onto me, impaling yourself on my thick pole, yours sitting proudly on my chest, throbbing, just like your ass as it spreads itself around my eager cock.

BACK OFF

After you have broken yourself in, you grab my hands and throw your legs on either side of my chest. It's a team effort now. I'm helping rock you back and forth, my inches wedged deep inside you, hard enough to make you wince each time you feel me all the way in but gently enough to keep you balanced on top of me and both of us on the board. You ride me, twisting your ass from side to side, letting off little moans each time you feel me sliding inside you, forcing your ass to spread wider apart for my destructive pole. I'm so turned on watching your tanned teenage body moving up and down on me, your big cock flopping around from in between your tan lines, taking turns smacking both our stomachs and leaving a sticky trail behind it.

Use teamwork to rock that boat
Intensity +++

Penetration: deep
Difficulty: hard

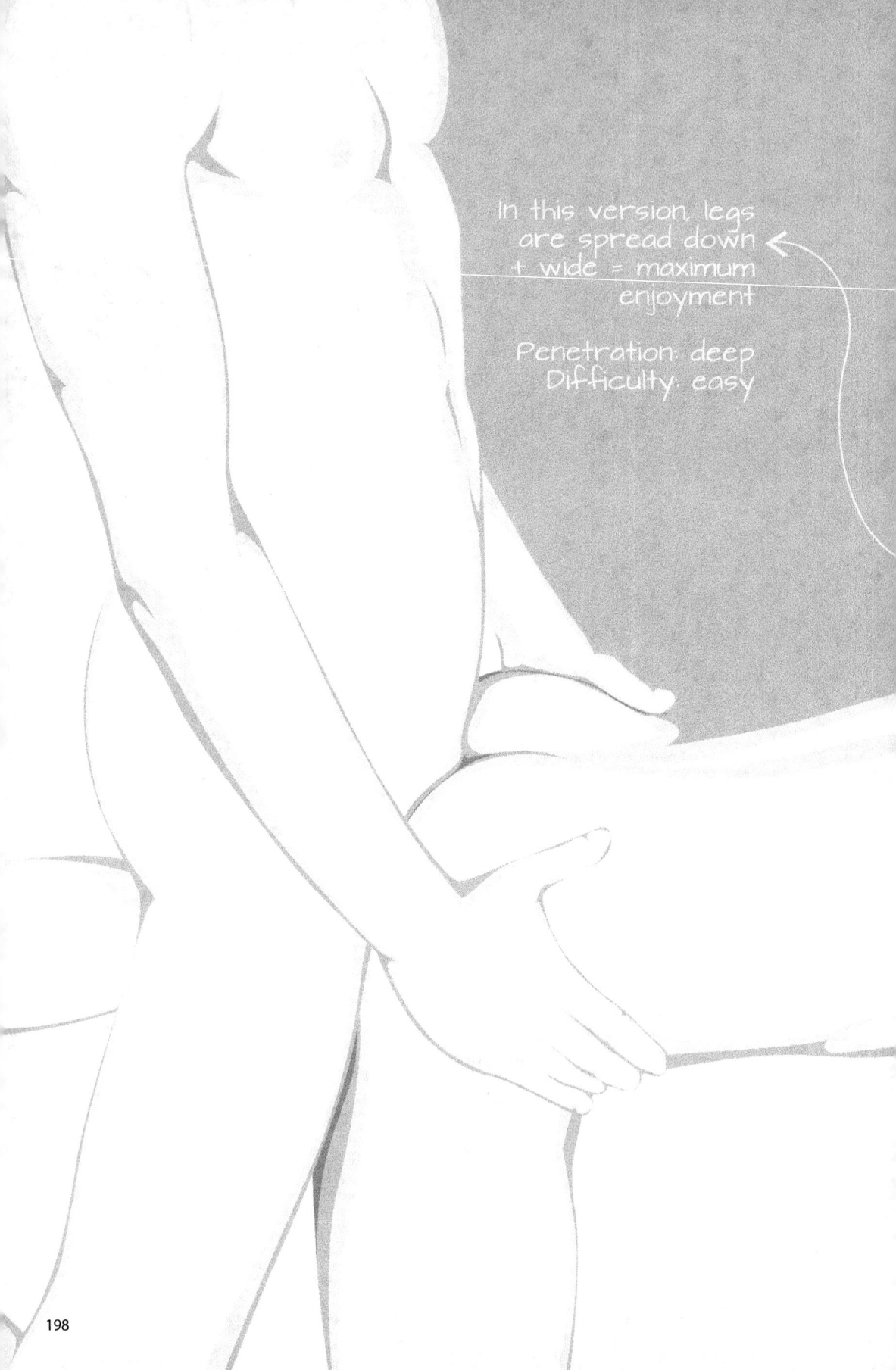

In this version, legs
are spread down ←
+ wide = maximum
enjoyment

Penetration: deep
Difficulty: easy

BACKDOOR

t's time we hit the beach, so I can really get into you. I have so much pleasure just throwing you face down on all fours and making you eat the sand, then I kneel down behind you and spread your ass wide. My thick bone is dripping wet, and forcibly presses between your cheeks. I spread you wide; to make sure you can feel me forcing myself into you. You let out short gasps, getting louder the deeper I go. "Take that, you little surfer!" I'm brutal with your little ass, gripping your hips with both hands and jamming you back onto my cock. I want to abuse that damn tight ass of yours, as it wraps itself around my thick inches. You scream out for more, as I relentlessly slam in and out of you, my low hanging balls slapping loudly up against you with each thrust. I can see you digging into the sand with both hands, begging me to go deeper.

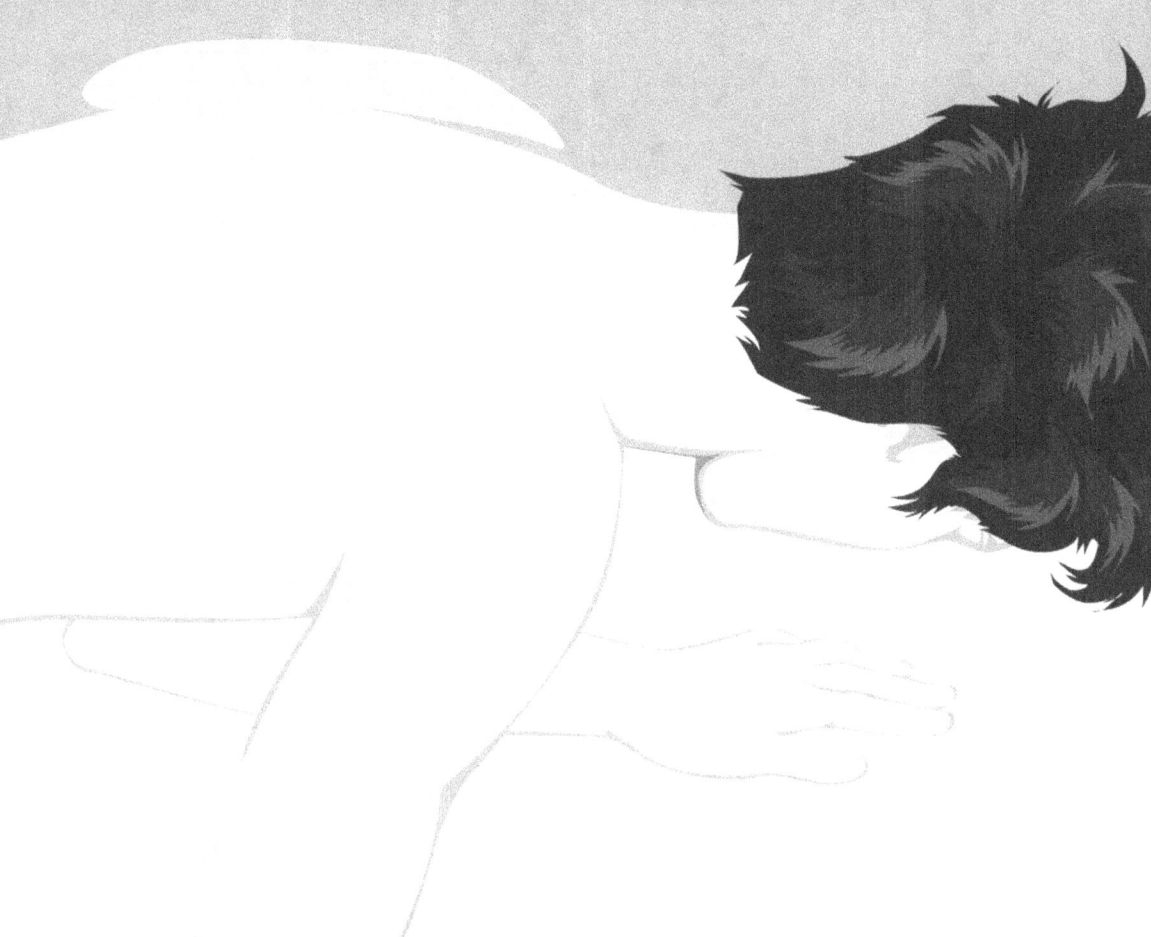

DROP KNEE

I want to feel you rear up onto me now, beach boy, push that juicy butt onto my ready and waiting inches, and continue to fuck my brains out. I lean back and watch you grind your ass up and down. I feel it swallowing every last bit of my cock. You thrust your hips hard and take control. I grab you by the waist and make you slam down on me fast and hard. I still feel and hear your raging hard-on smacking around, throwing sand everywhere. Sweat covers your smooth body; it feels so good as I run my hand down your tanned back and gently smack your hot little butt.

Rough riding + hard thrusting

Penetration: deep
Difficulty: hard

THRUSTER

The beach is lined with dunes that I've been wanting to bend you up against. With one leg up and reaching over to touch your toes, you let me watch you open up for me. From behind, I have an awesome view of your lean, sand covered butt, bent and spread, eager for what's coming next. I run a few fingers around your sticky hole and toy with it for a bit, making the little blond hairs on your cheeks stand up. But there's something else—as you're about to find out—standing up behind you, waiting to thrash you repeatedly until you're begging me to stop. You're not nearly as out of breath as I'd expected, in fact, you're begging for more. The energy and willingness of a teenage surfer with his legs spread in the sand, glistening in the heat of the afternoon sun is beyond intoxicating. Well, I have got plenty more for you to ride surfer boy.

Simple + sexy
Visually intoxicating!
Sex on the beach is
fucking hot!

Penetration: medium
Difficulty: medium

As the name suggests -
Hard + intense +++ deep +++

Penetration: deep
Difficulty: hard

DRILLING

You want deeper? Let me throw you onto one of the beach chairs and show you what a real drilling feels like. From behind and underneath you, I can stuff every inch of my thick cock up into you—and own that ass like you've never been owned before. I pump your ass furiously and smack your tight cheeks in turn, just to remind you who's in control. Your little ass is well worn by now and willingly takes my throbbing knob as far deep as it will go.

Your legs start to shake, as I teach you first-hand what the real meaning of "pain and pleasure" is all about. I feel your body tense, and your ass starts to pulse wildly around my throbbing pole. Your massive load shoots up and hits you in the face, before it starts to drip down your lips into your mouth. Impressed with your effort, you slide off my cock and turn and press your lips up against mine, so I can share your thick, salty juice as you let it dribble down onto my tongue.

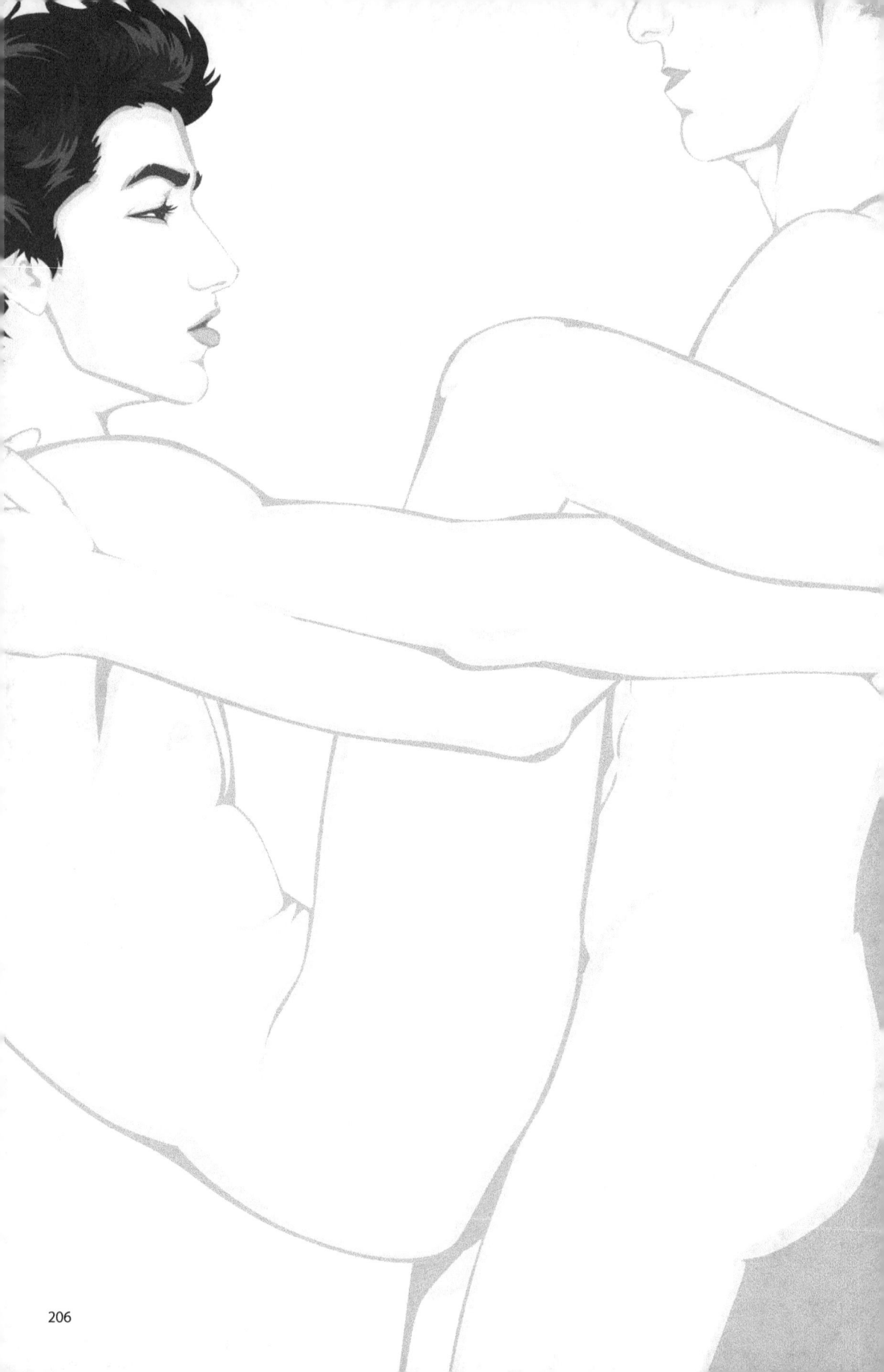

Only for the upper body fit - carrying your boy around is the ultimate ownership!

Penetration: deep +++
Difficulty: hard +++

HANG TEN

I want to return the favor and give you a load back—just the way you like it, eight-plus inches deep. Though I'm going to make it feel more like nine by the time your legs are thrown up over my shoulders and I'm holding you up, spread and thrusting into you. Soon my cock is so deep up inside you, your body goes limp and you just hang there, staring up at me, short of breath. I hold nothing back as I slam you over and over again. Suddenly, without warning, I'm gushing torrents inside you. I hold it in there long enough so that you can't take another drop, then feel you slide your legs down and tangle them around mine, throwing me face down into the sand beside you. You jump on top of me and slap me a couple of times with your half soft, but still amazingly long dick. Maybe it's time to flip?

GROUPSEX —
TO LIFT YOU
TRY A NEW

A BOLD WAY
R GAME &
POSITION

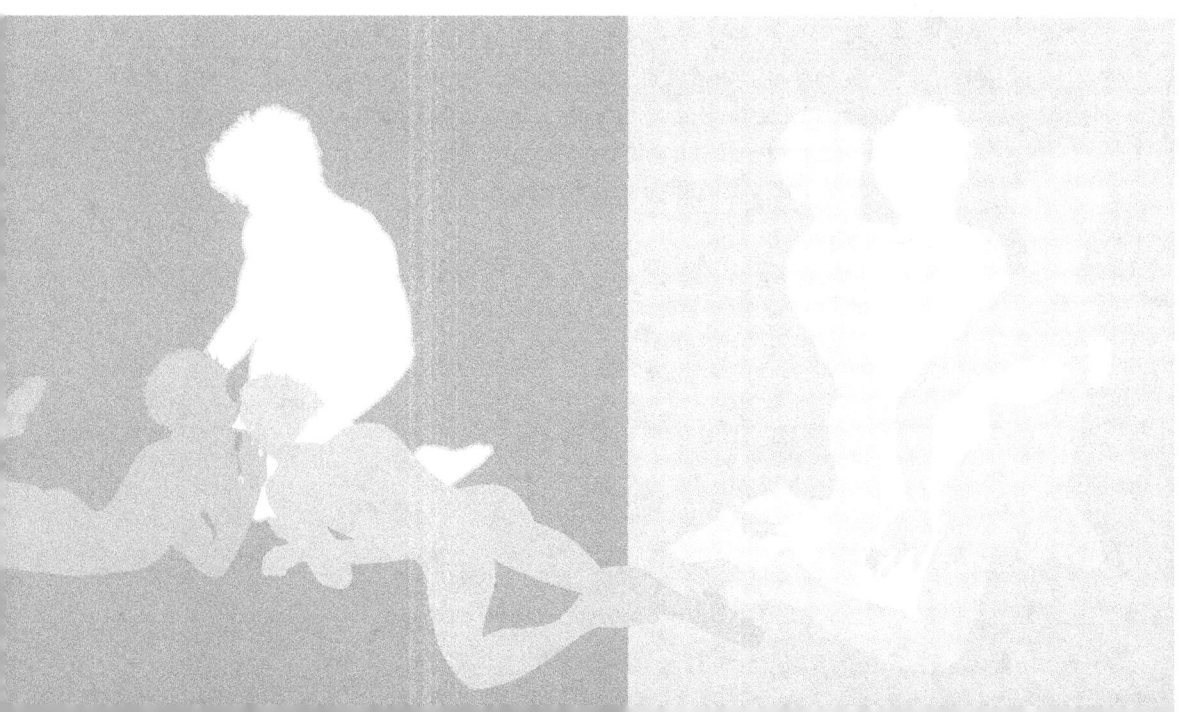

CHAPTER 13

WEIGHTLIFTING

Spotting you at the gym as you pushed weights was a great workout by itself. I enjoyed standing over you and dominating you with the heavyweight bars. On your last sets you would always need my help lifting them up off your chest. Occasionally I would enjoy letting the weights pin you down a little, my crotch in your face in loose gym shorts with nothing on underneath. As you were struggling on your last few reps, breathing heavily under the weight of the bar I was pinning you down with, I would bend my knees just enough to feel your breath on my thick uncut meat, as I pressed the inside of my shorts against the side of your face.

Despite struggling to breathe and being unable to move, the outline of your cut teenage knob was furiously pressing up against your tight gym shorts. Unable to hide that you're actually enjoying being dominated by your sweating mate at the gym, you look up at me as I continue to hold you down until I see the outline in your shorts moisten, and then I know you're ready to be rewarded for your lifting efforts.

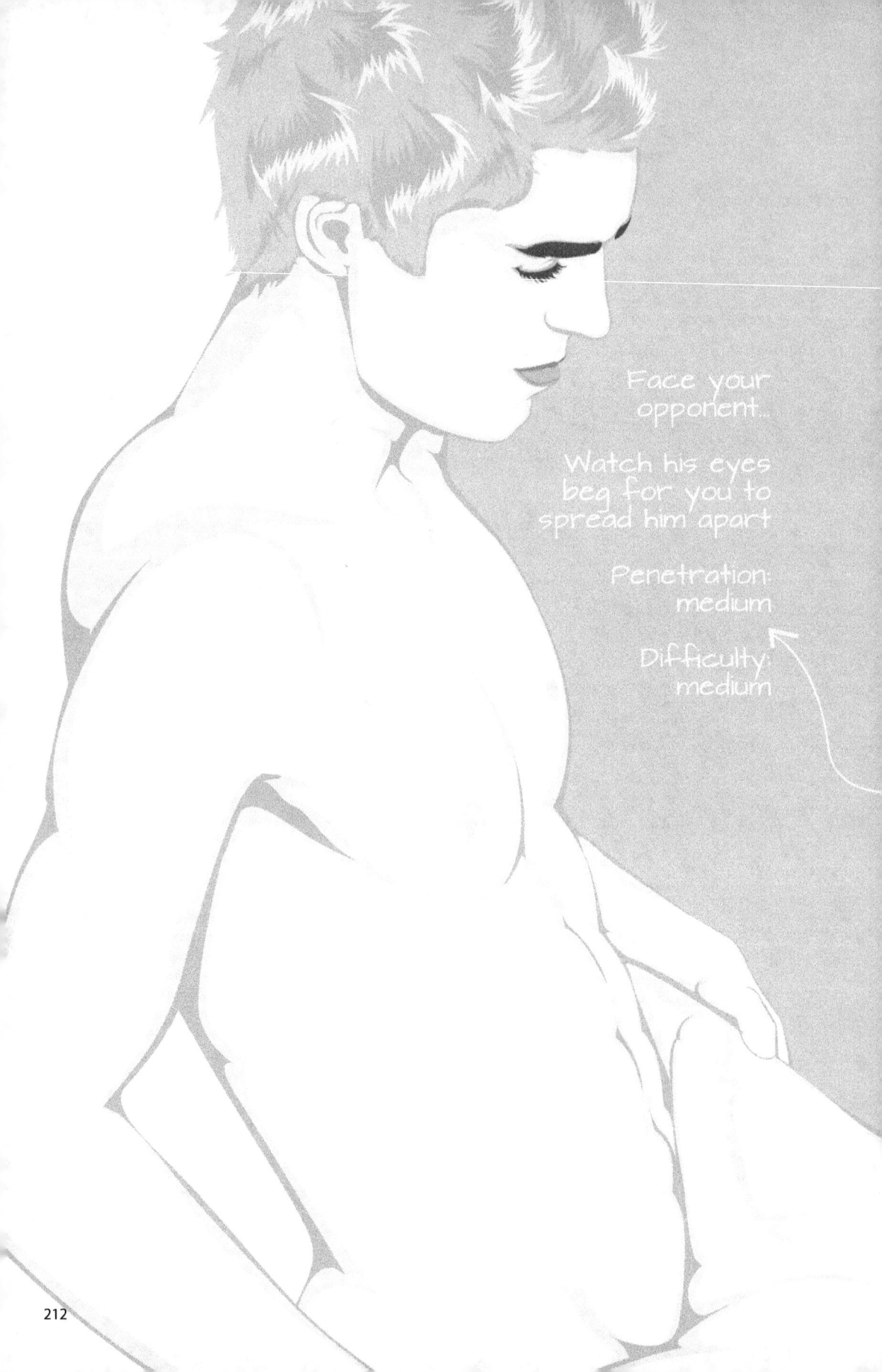

Face your
opponent...

Watch his eyes
beg for you to
spread him apart

Penetration:
medium

Difficulty:

JERK GRIP

Still on your back I spin you around to the side of the bench and kneel down between your legs. Taking my cue, you gladly peel your shorts off and drop them to the floor till you're lying naked from the waist down, wearing nothing but a loose fitting gym singlet, which is barely able to hide the eagerness of your proud teenage bar of meat standing straight up and glistening with excitement. I grab your legs and spread them wide, running my hands up the inside of your thighs and sliding one, then two fingers into your already moistening ass. From where I'm kneeling my big cock is already rock hard and just inches from the hole it's about to penetrate. I use my fingers to spread you open and slide my cock inside, making sure you feel every inch of me throbbing deep inside you.

LEG THRUST

You don't want to hold back an inch. Quickly standing up in front of me, you rub your slowly dripping knob against my lips, driving the taste and smell of teenage excitement into my mouth and making me grow even bigger and harder. You forcefully throw me onto my back and take charge, dropping your body into a full squat right down onto me until you're impaled to the core on my bar. My bare knob is shoved so deep in you I feel it grinding against your insides, and you waste no time abusing my raw cock, tearing up and down on it, the sound of your hard meat slapping loudly against your chest, like a free weight falling heavily onto the ground.

Simple + sexy + hot
Designed to satisfy the cravings of both playmates

Penetration: deep
Difficulty: medium

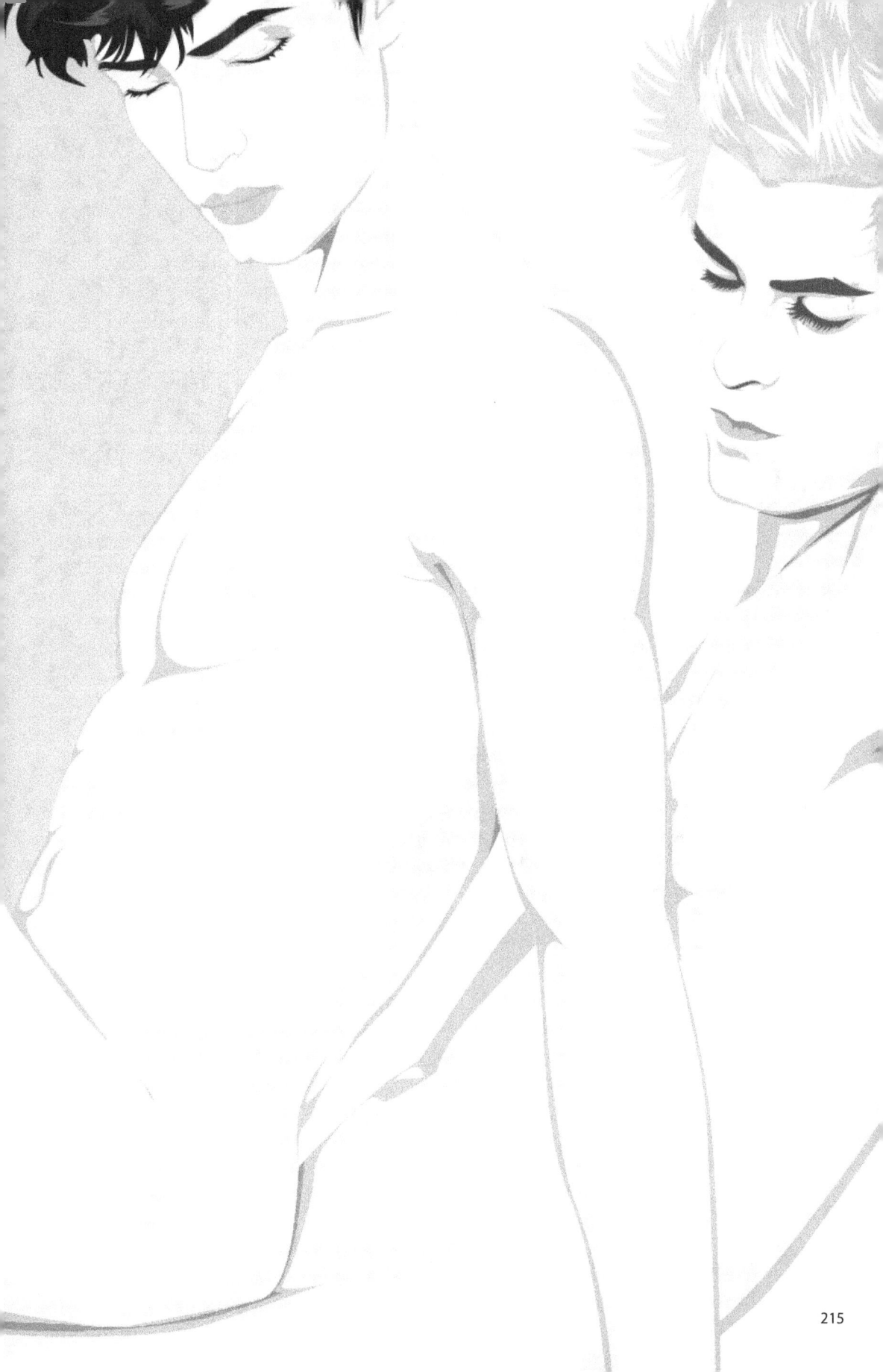

Bored at work?
Try this kitsch number out in the
boardroom after hours.

Penetration: deep
Difficulty: medium

KNEE TOUCH

t's only a small gym, and the trainer has a great little desk off in the corner. I've often thought of sitting back on that cozy looking chair, a cute ass in my lap riding my cock. You're chafing my cock beyond belief with that hungry ass, and when I plunge it back inside where it belongs, I'm firmly grabbing onto your waist and forcing you as far down as it will go. As I keep power-fucking you, pulling you down hard; your ass suddenly begins to contract, nearly tearing me apart, and I know you're about to blow. I wrap my hand around your long cock and jerk it hard until it swells. Suddenly, you're blowing everywhere, painting my hand and the insides of your legs with your thick load, the stench of your teenage cum overpowering every one of my senses.

CLEAN AND JERK

As I force you back onto the floor and spread your legs apart, I cover my cock with the dirty load dripping off my hand and use it to lube me up so I can shove every last bit of my meat right where it belongs. Slamming hard, I force your cum back inside you, my massive balls slapping loudly against your ass, beating you up as you moan with sheer pleasure. You grab my balls and squeeze them. I didn't realize what you were doing until you suddenly ripped my cock out of your hole and pushed my left testicle inside instead. As my ball slides into your ass, a sharp pain suddenly consumes me and runs all the way up my cock. Balls are not meant to be jammed into boys' holes, but the intensifying swelling is only making me stiffer as the throbbing increases.

FULL EXTENSION

t's a team effort all the way as I stand up and hold your long legs spread wide on either side of me. It gives me the best view of your ass, as I penetrate it violently. Obediently down on your hands in front of me puts me in control, and I like taking charge and making you do as you're told. Teenagers like you deserve to be dominated. I slam you fast and hard, the way you like it, and watch my thick inches slide in and out of your well-worked hole. After a final thrust I pull out and spill my pole inside your cheeks my load so thick, it paints your gaping hole entirely. I use my sticky knob to push more of my thick cum back inside you, and start to fuck you with it again.

Get down on all 'twos' teenager!
And let me make you climb the walls

Penetration deep
Difficulty: hard ++

221

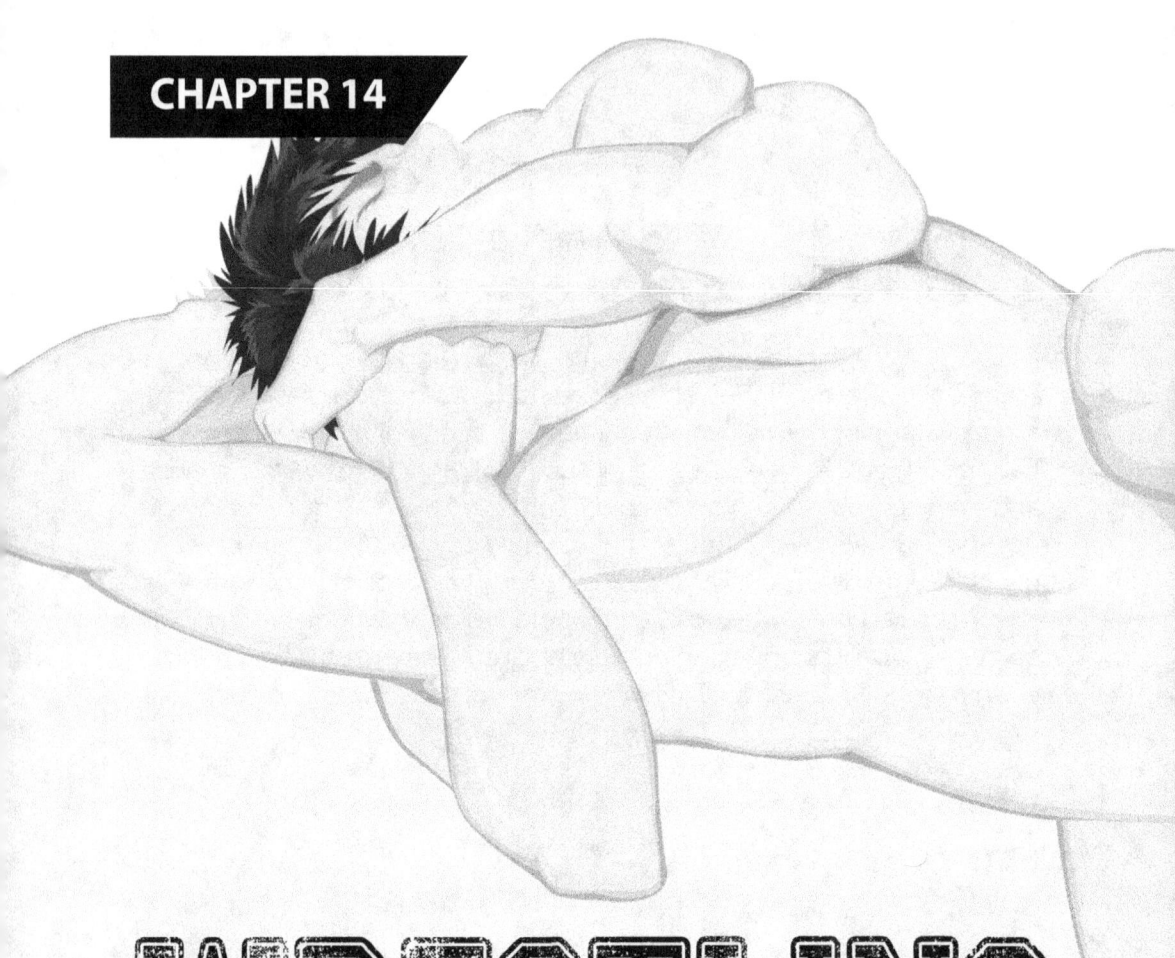

CHAPTER 14

WRESTLING

"Date" night at my place on a work night might have been a pretty relaxed way to hang out and spend some time with you. But when my keen sense of sexual aggression, mixed with a couple days' worth of sexual frustration, got the better of me, the tide turned. Throw some beers, pizza and a movie into the mix, and it was actually a decadent way of spending a night in. Suffice to say that watching you sit next to me, in a pair of boxers and a loose hoodie, on the oversized beanbag was enough to make me want to throw you around the room ten times over. The way you sat with your legs spread in your loose fitting boxers teased me to the point of frustration. I could see exactly how this date night was going to end, and I was pretty sure it would involve you, butt naked and gasping for air, topped off with my cum dripping down the side of that pretty little face of yours.

DUCK UNDER

First things first, though. I press closer to you and run my hand up the inside of your boxers, bringing about an almost instant hard-on, one of the things I love most about your teenage cock. I rip off the shorts and throw my legs on either side of you, lying back and pushing my package straight up into your face. You don't waste a second. Sliding your tongue out and around my thick knob, you go straight to work sucking on it and taking it further into your mouth, an inch at a time, just the way I like it. This is far from over, though, and you're about to get knocked to the ground like you can't even imagine.

Lock your legs in + push that head down
playmate's faces were made for this

Difficulty: medium

BODY PRESS

'm really in the mood to beat you up with my throbbing inches, and I definitely intend to make date night this week anything but slow-paced. I wrestle you to the ground and roll around with you, making sure to lose the rest of our clothes in the process. When I finally have you pinned down, rubbing your face into the carpet in a half-nelson, I flip you over onto your back, where you belong. Staring down at you from above, your legs spread and wrapped around me, I enjoy watching every one of your facial expressions as I press up against you and plunge deep. The look of pleasant surprise on your face simply begs me to go further, until your eyes are rolling back in your head, a perfect mix of both pleasure and pain.

Sensual + intimate + intense
Watch his eyes plead for more...

Penetration: deep
Difficulty: easy

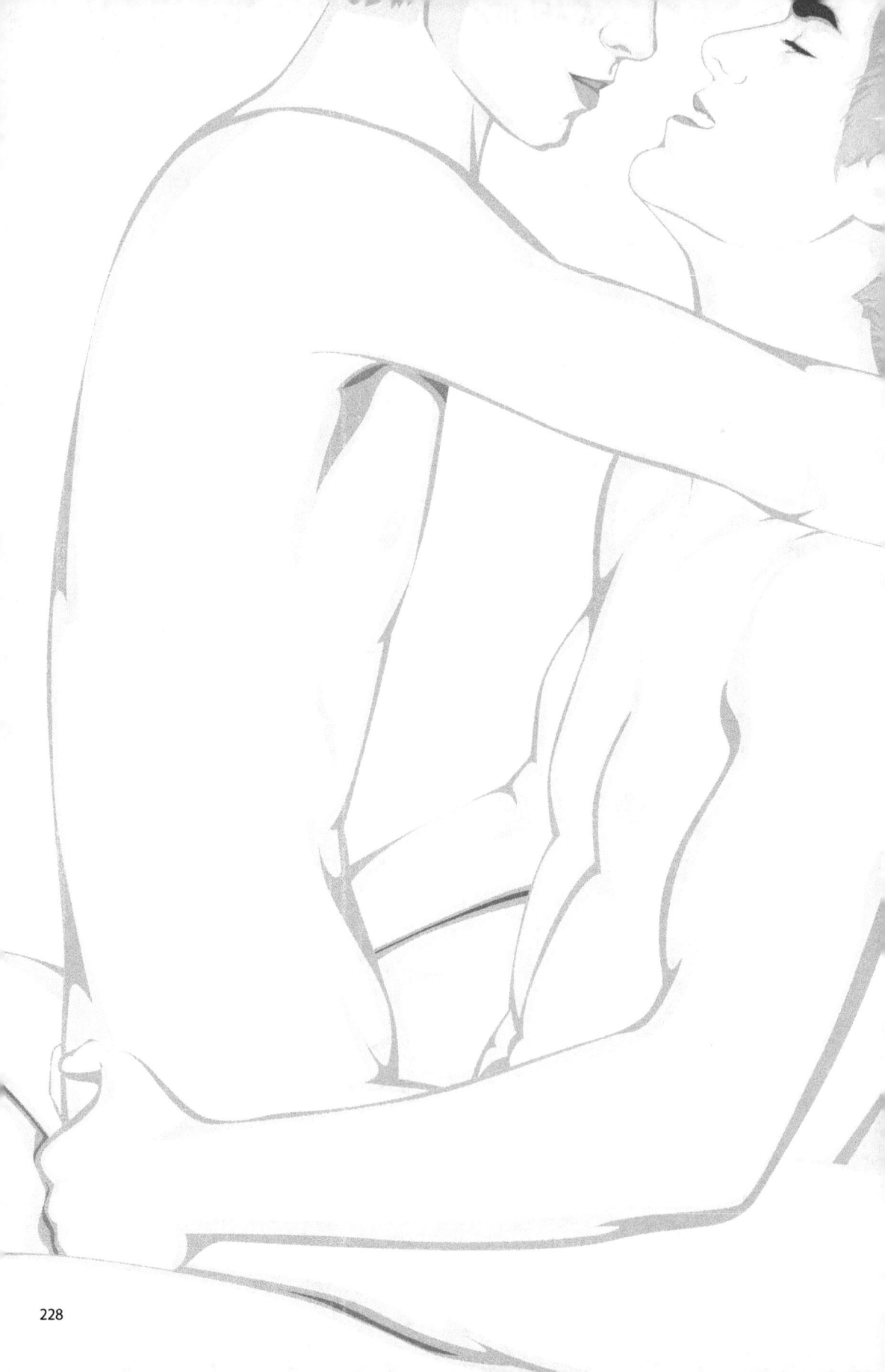

*Breaking him in?
Try this on for size..
Bottom playmate in complete
control here - can go as
slow or deep as he wants!*

*Penetration: medium
Difficulty: easy*

CRADLE

A wild, sex-hungry look in your eye begins to glow as the aggressive teenager I love suddenly leans up and puts me into a headlock, this time forcing me to the ground. Without warning, your ass violently jams down onto my cock, nearly knocking the breath out of me. Feeling you sliding so intensely down on top of me, holding your ass spread apart and letting me sit inside you, gets me so rock hard, there's no saying how long I could stay in there. You lean down and put your tongue into my mouth so I can feel your lips against mine and your short, sharp breaths pushing down into my throat. You bite my lower lip as you grind down on me harder, making sure you can feel the entire length and thickness of my knob doing you damage.

TAKEDOWN

Stay on top of me and keep riding that cock! You grab my hands and take me down until I'm flat on my back and you're on top and completely in control. I can feel your palms sweating intensely. You squeeze hard, as the feeling of my thick cock tearing into you continues to flood your teenage body. It sends shivers down your spine as you throw your head back and scream my name, your toes curling from the intense stimulation, leaving your body drenched in sweat.

Knees bent =
greater thrust
for both
Feel his palms
sweat, as you
plunge deep

Penetration: deep
Difficulty: medium

FULL NELSON

You're being fucked so hard now, I don't think I would even let you tap out of this round. I want to take a turn from behind and feel your body lying up against mine. I wrestle you back to the ground where I can shove two fingers straight into you and watch you squirm. By the time I slam you down onto the coffee table, you're eagerly anticipating being pulled down on top of my inches again, until each one is all the way in you. Your back is curved to press your ass as tight against me as you can, and I've locked my arms around your chest for total control and deep penetration. Your body belongs to me now and was meant to have me dominating you. The short, sharp thrusts make you wince each time, and let me know that I'm penetrating you to the core.

Intensity + passion locked in
Pull down hard for slow, deliberate thrusts..

Penetration: deep
Difficulty: medium

FIREMAN'S CARRY

My heart's racing, and the pressure in between my legs intensifies. Realizing I'm not too far from my massive load painting your insides, I pull out of you and slide a few fingers back in till I hear you whining my name. Covered in sweat, you're screaming at me to fuck you again, and I can't help but lean you up on the chair and stand behind you, then push my swollen cock straight back into your gaping hole, where it belongs.

Standing tall this time makes for smoother sailing.
Fit for a first timer!

Penetration: medium
Difficulty: easy

CROTCH LIFT

t's the passionate final round now and I feel you wrap your legs around me for one last time. I aggressively lift you up by the crotch and force myself inside, making it perfectly clear that you never forget who that piece of ass belongs to. It's time to pay you with every last drop for being such a formidable opponent. Getting off on the scent of your arousal, together with the stifled moans on which you're choking, it's my last stand, and as my balls continue to slap your ass, I feel them suddenly tighten and my knob expand. I feel your nails dig into my back as you feel what's coming. I let loose, my load uncontrollably pouring into you. I feel the grip of your hands on the back of my neck tighten, as you feel me fill you with everything I've got.

The most intimate part of our sexual bond is being able to slam you back onto the ground and stay there, inside you, for hours after I'm done with you. Not only does the look of sheer ecstasy on your face give me such intense pleasure, it runs even deeper than that. There are nights I have sex dreams about impaling you that are so intense, I wake up in a hot sweat. I lie awake in bed craving for the next chance I can force myself between your legs, spread them apart and make sure you feel every inch of my intense hunger, teaching you over and over again everything there is to know about the language of sex.

I can't wait to make you taste the banana smoothies I have in store for you next time we meet.

There's nothing practical about this position, despite being erotic, sensual and just plain sexy to watch.

Maybe it's time to invite a third?

Penetration: deep
Difficulty: hard

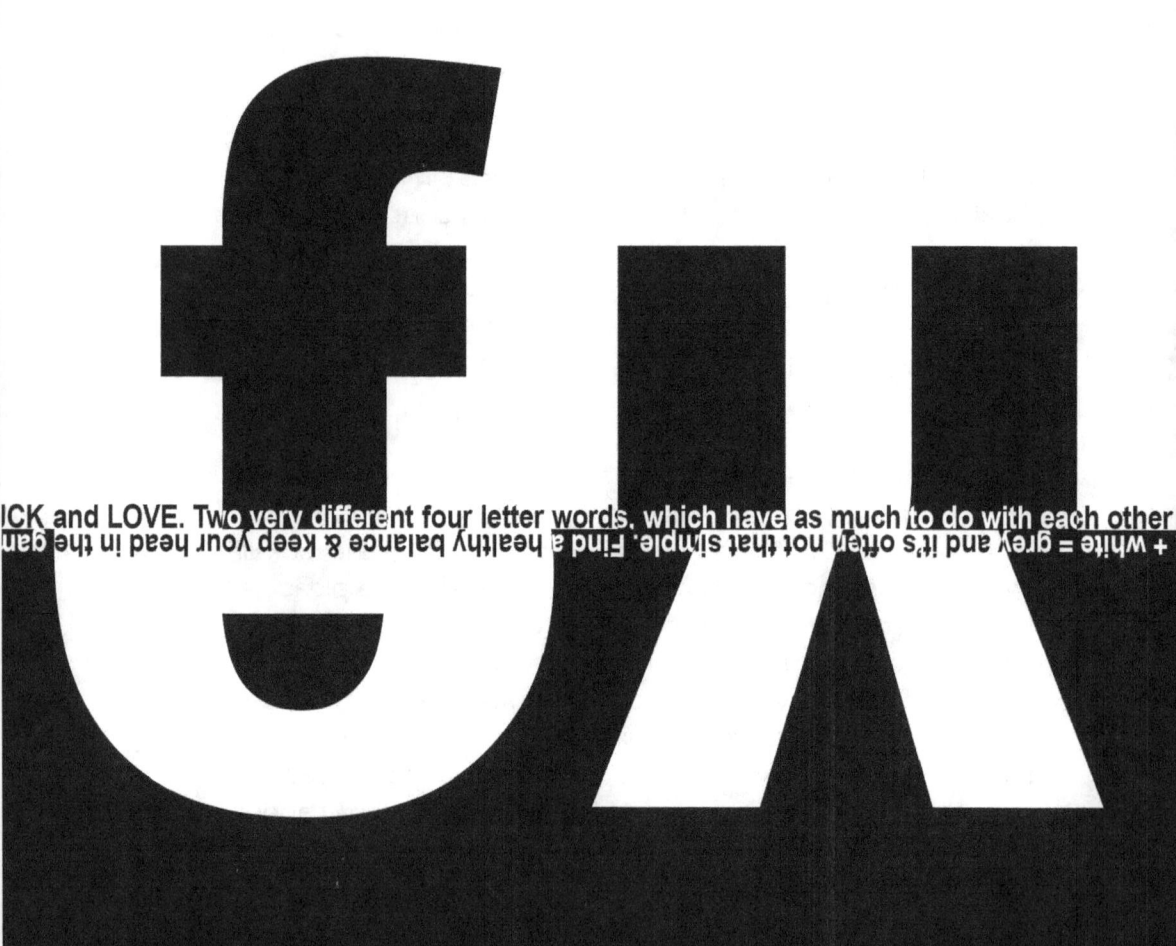

UCK and LOVE. Two very different four letter words, which have as much to do with each other

k + white = grey and it's often not that simple. Find a healthy balance & keep your head in the gam

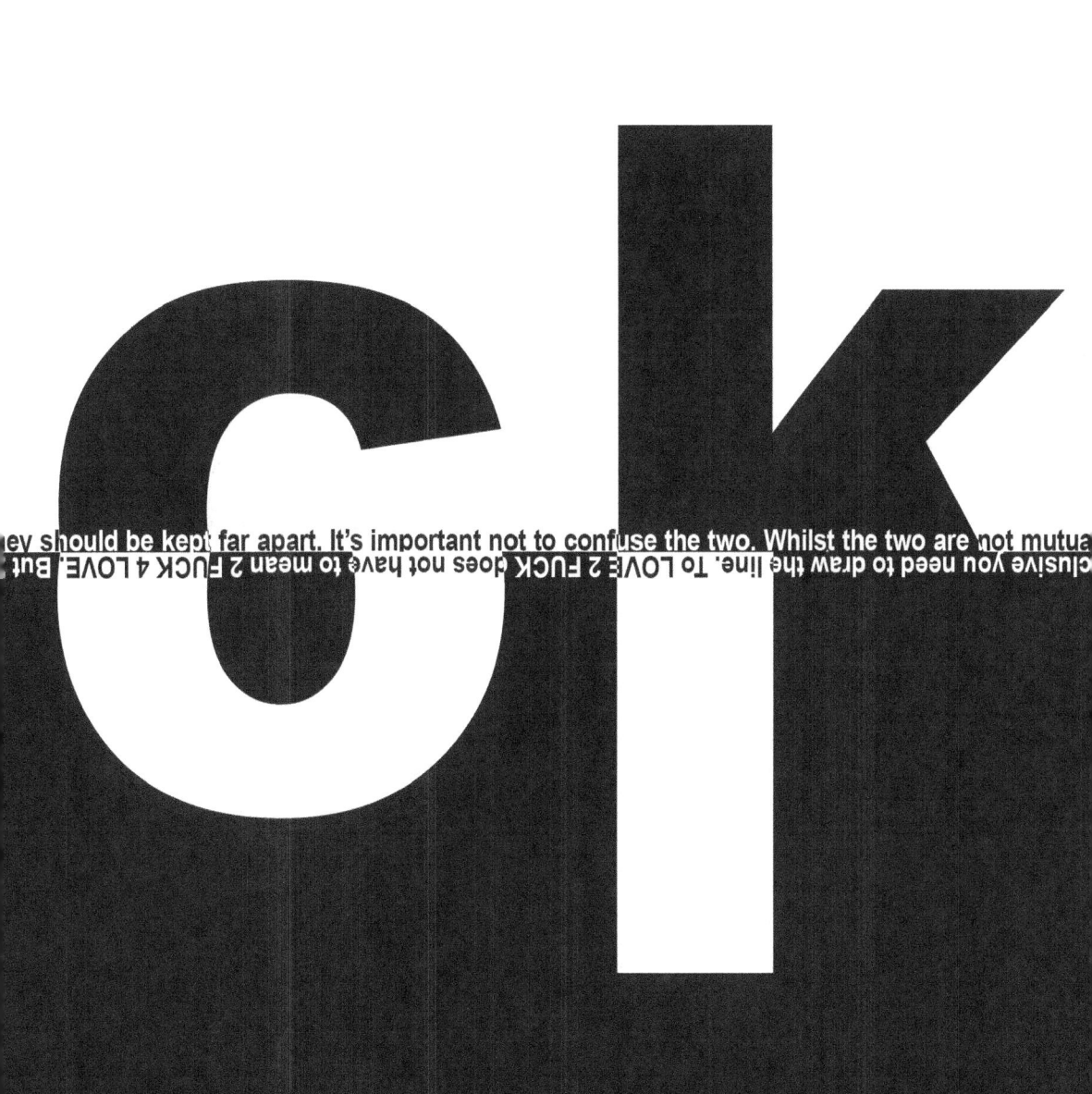

ey should be kept far apart. It's important not to confuse the two. Whilst the two are not mutua
clusive you need to draw the line. To LOVE 2 FUCK does not have 2 mean 2 FUCK 4 LOVE. But

#22

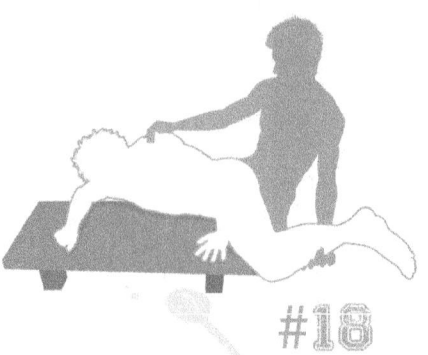

#18

#26

BASEBALL

Score Card

#16

#24

#20

#30

#36

BASKETBALL
ScoreCard

#32

#34

#38

#46

#52

#56

BOXING
ScoreCard

#54

#50

#48

#72

#68

CRICKET
ScoreCard

#66

#62

#70

DIVING
ScoreCard

#80

#82

#78

#88

#84

#86

#100

#94

FOOTBALL
ScoreCard

#96

#102

#92

#98

#104

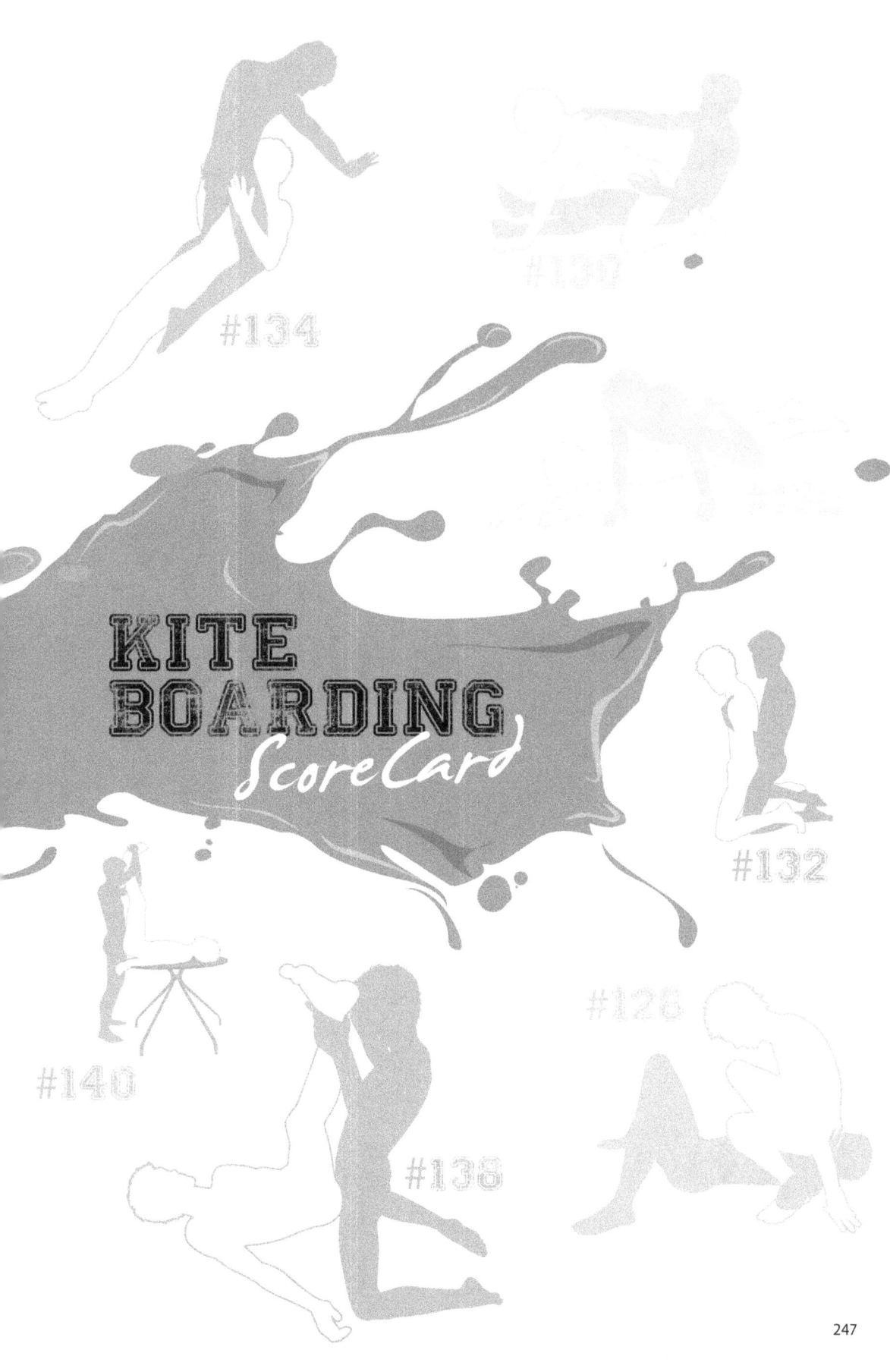

#156

#154

NFL
Scorecard

#148

#152

#158

#150

#146

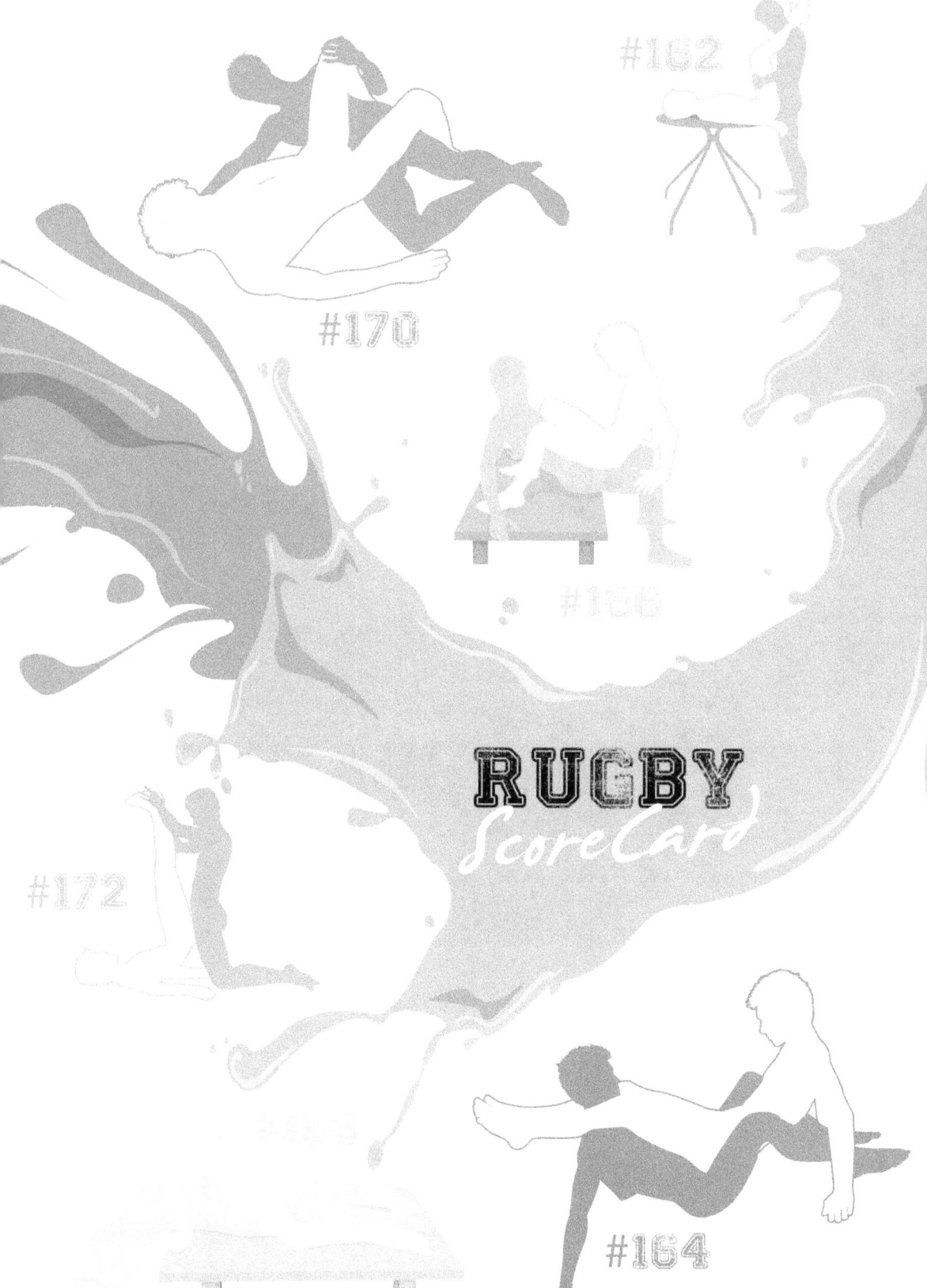

#162

#170

#166

RUGBY
ScoreCard

#172

#164

#190

#184

#182

SNOWBOARDING
ScoreCard

#178

#180

#202

#200

#206

#204

SURFING
ScoreCard

#194

#196

#218

#214

WEIGHTLIFTING
Scorecard

#220

#212

#226

WRESTLING

#234

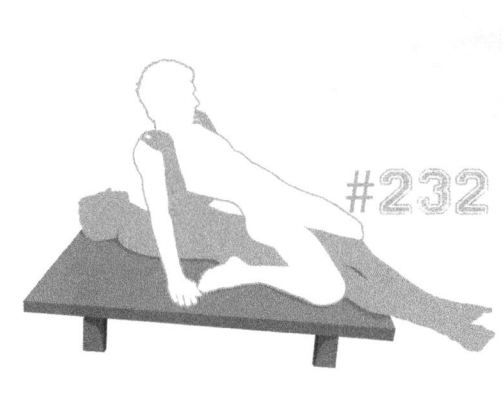

#232

#224

ACKNOWLEDGEMENTS

Life, like sex is a constant journey and one that involves countless personal and working relationships to keep everything in check. It's often a skillful combination of both, and as with all skills in life they require constant development.

It gives me great pleasure to be able to say "Thank You" to everyone who has (patiently) stood by my side on both levels, contributed to my personal growth and pushed me to achieve my potential. I'm grateful to a lot of people who have driven and inspired the creation of the Kaleb Sutra – the publication of this first installment and the ongoing efforts to release the remaining installments and the overall volume in the coming year.

As each of you is well aware, despite a sincere desire to see life in black and white, I'm often very comfortable (and complacent) in finding myself somewhere in the middle (and I don't think even "50 shades of grey" would be enough at times to cover all the "grey area" that goes on in all of life's deeply satisfying, however challenging, tangle of relationships).

I appreciate every one of you more than words can possibly express, and I do hope that this (fast-growing) "few words" will get across as much.

M: Perhaps the biggest driving force in inspiring me to embrace myself and do it well. The journey has been a long and often uphill battle, but you have stuck with me throughout and motivated me to arrange my jumble of writing styles on the page in the right way. (Oh, and, of course, for proof-reading the text with me enough times to likely be able to recite the entire book from memory by now!)

A: Over the past year, the insights and constructive criticisms that you have applied to the production of this first and upcoming installments have been invaluable, and your behind the scenes support has allowed me to finally stand tall and see all of my ambitions through a fresh perspective.

Thanks to my loyal teammates. Each one of you has put out a solid round and, as you know, it's almost always guaranteed to be a rough ride.

Marie: Your design ability and patience over the past months to collaborate this first installment have been outstanding, and I thank you for all of your hard work and look forward to producing each language adaptation and knocking over the next few books with you.

Scott: Thanks for assisting me throughout the proofing and editing process and smoothing out any "writer's blocks," which we know can be at times cumbersome.

Of course, this list would not be complete without acknowledging every one of you that have made it this far and are reading this. My journey over the past five, six, seven.... years would not have been possible without your encouraging words, fan base and excitement from my rookie years on XTube.

Thanks for sticking it out with me, one load at a time. I'm here to stay and can't wait to share every bit of me with every one of you.

Erotic capital is the way of the world and speaks true, down to the very last drop.

"Everything in the world is about sex, except sex.
Sex is about power" – Oscar Wilde

***

So take your positions and let's get started on the second round. Sexy has never tasted this good. Banana smoothie anyone?

What does your banana
smoothie taste like?

THE BEST TASTING SEX IS YET TO COME. KC

THE FINAL WHISTLE

These are two people that I haven't had the opportunity to meet, but have provided me with great inspiration and positive reinforcement towards achieving my goals in life.

Inspiration is all around us and I hope that you all find time to read, travel and explore new things in life, in order to find those people who inspire you...

RICHARD BRANSON: I don't think I need to say too much besides that I'm starting to get what it's all about. The more I've grown up in recent years, the greater my appreciation of your lust for life has become. Thank YOU for being one of the few people who has what it takes to inspire me to have the drive and determination to achieve great things in life, and I do hope to one day have the opportunity to kite board off Necker Is. with you.

In the spirit of this, my first published book, which is an achievement I intend to hang my hat on, I leave on a positive note conveyed by yours truly:

> "Above all, you want to create something you're proud of. This has always been my philosophy of business."

PS. Having spent thousands of hours flying, and as a complete airline nerd... Thank you for giving me one of the best experiences I have had in-flight to date on board a 2011 trans-Atlantic flight to O'Hare. When I worked a brief stint for the Virgin Blue group in Australia in my teenage years, I honestly hadn't the slightest that I would be scrawling to you, in the back of my first book some years later! It seems that red was indeed the new blue.

TABATHA COFFEY: I understand full well that 'It's not really about the hair', and as a fellow blond from down under, who's moral-heavy sense of upbringing has forced my hand at a long-ass journey of self-discovery, conflicting-values and more internal-battles along the way than I care to even remember – I respect you a lot. Your poise and grace and intellectual handling of situations has been a breath of fresh air and taught me that rather than fighting against the world, there's ways to approach life in a much more 'professional' and cerebral way. I'd love to get the chance to sit in your chair one day and have you tell it like it is. I'll bring the Vegemite.

www.ingramcontent.com/pod-product-compliance
Lightning Source LLC
Chambersburg PA
CBHW081227020726
47503CB00011B/2938